Alicia Howard Presents

STREET BITCHES DON'T NEED LOVE!

By

Alicia Howard

Alicia Howard Presents

STREET BITCHES DON'T NEED LOVE!

Alicia Howard Presents

CHAPTER 1

As the car sped down the highway, rap music blasts from the speakers.

Hurricane aka Heather head bangs against the trunk of her husband's car. I know this blowing your mind. Hurricane is not a saint her mouth is reckless, which causes some to call her Heat.

She is beaten, raped, and shot a twice, yet she still fighting for life thinking of how she even got here.

Hurricane's father Harvey the called him Heavy. He is not a big man in appearance. However, his name carries huge weight in the drug game. Heavy was

Alicia Howard Presents

a major kingpin who started in Saint Louis then relocated himself and his hustle to Chicago where he met Hurricane's mother.

After Heavy married Hurricane's mother, he moved on to a bigger part of the drug trade in New York. Heavy pushed heroin the deadliest drug known to man. Fiends will kill you to get it, a nigga will pretend he loves you to get it, and bitch will set you up to get it

Hurricane thought about her dad fades. Her body hurt badly from the damage her husband and six of his friends put on her pussy and asshole. She feels blood trickling down her legs.

Alicia Howard Presents

Hurricane saw none of this coming her way. She knows her father rolling over in his grave.

Heavy told her never trust a fuck nigga. He even taught her how to spot one a mile away. As Hurricane, battered body bangs from side to side to side. She could hear her father saying, *"Heather you're all I got. Your mommy died to give me you. It not your time fight for your life."* Heavy taught her to be strong she doesn't know how she fell victim to this shit. Hurricane thought about the story of her birth.

Alicia Howard Presents

*Hurricane's mother gave birth,
Hurricane father had to pick whom he
would save. Heavy gave her mother
enough happiness for ten women lifetime.
Yet the baby did not have a fair chance.
Heavy kissed his wife goodbye then told
the doctor to save his baby.*

Hurricane keeps going in and out of consciousness yet she heard father saying, *"If a man hates on another nigga that is doing better than him. That is a fuck nigga. A man that depends on a woman is a fuck nigga. A man that lies about his sex game is a fuck nigga. Any man that hits a woman is a fuck nigga.*

Any nigga that rolls over on his friend is a fuck nigga."

Hurricane's husband is guilty of a few of these except for the hitting because she is not the bitch for that. If Taz pulled that, he would be the muthafucka in this trunk.

Taz display characteristic of a fuck nigga. Most stood out to her occurred a week ago.

Taz comes home huffing Hurricane asks, "Taz what's the matter?"

Initially he acts as if he did not want to talk about it. Then Taz told her his best friend Mark is fucking with the work and money. Hurricane did not believe him.

Once Mark left town she knew that something up. Taz did not tell Hurricane the truth. It was strange to her all the years she has known Mark, he just did not seem to be the type to steal, hide, or run.

Hurricane chuckles she doesn't know the nigga she married. However, she is trying to pinpoint another muthafucka personality. Truth is she knows who Taz is she over look things he did.

Alicia Howard Presents

Taz tries to play the big man. He always makes the team believe they work for him knowing they work for Hurricane. Taz would talk shit like *"Niggas will always respect my queen."*

One nigga called him on the shit saying *"It's not because of you Hurricane gets respect."* Taz got mad he beat that boy into a coma.

Hurricane questioned Taz about the issue his response *"I am not jealous of your legacy baby that dude did not respect my gangsta."*

Hurricane lying in the back of this trunk told her just how real the jealousy between her and Taz is. She is dying to get out the fucking truck. The gas fumes make her sick partly because she pregnant.

Hurricane had not told Taz because they lost so many babies she did not want to jinx this one. Also, Taz did not think kids fit their lifestyle. Hurricane planned to tell him when the baby almost on the way.

The trauma her body endured over the last twenty-four hours. Hurricane knew the baby long gone. A tear rolls down her cheek at the thought. The car came to a stop so fast Hurricane's head

hits the jack lying back there with her.

Hurricane knocked out cold as she

went out. She prays she is on the way to

heaven to be with her parents

Taz jumps out the car in a wooded

area of Amagansett, NY. The population

is a thousand people. Taz knew

Hurricane would lie in the woods and

decay before anyone found her. It is late

fall too cold to hang outside, take walks,

and shit.

Chapter 2

Craig grabs Hurricane by the legs he is glad to help. He often tried to get pussy from Hurricane by telling her Taz cheats. Hurricane knew Taz cheats that is the reason she allows Craig to eat the pussy a few times.

Hurricane would act as if she felt bad, stopping him before going all the way never before she got that nut, believe that.

Craig felt Hurricane stupidity allowed this nigga to play her. If she had a nigga like him this would have never happened. He did not mind walking in her shadow unlike Taz who wants to walk in her shoes.

Craig feels Hurricane getting what the fuck she deserves. She picked the wrong nigga. Breeze looks at the setup he could not even believe he is a part of this. He never touched Hurricane because he has too much respect for her.

Hurricane is good people Taz did not have shit before Hurricane came in to his life.

He got her, acting as if he were the boss of some shit. The nigga was getting the boss's car wash when bumped into Hurricane washing her own car. She

would not give him any play at the car
wash.

Taz begs his boss to keep the car for
a week. He hunted her down like a
bloodthirsty dog that could not live
without her.

Now here they are harming the
person that fed all of them. Breeze shook
his head; he closes his eyes because the
battered mess he sees before him is not
Hurricane.

She five foot four, one hundred
sixty-eight pounds, the color of Almond
Butter, breast perky, stomach tight, nice
hips, just enough ass to keep a man

happy, short Blonde wavy hair and signature gray eyes she gotten from her mother.

Breeze was friends with Hurricane when her father was alive. He would say, *"Boy if you can get a woman with eyes like that, you a cold muthafucka."* He knew that Breeze was sweet on Hurricane. He also knew that Breeze's shyness would cause her to look over him. Hurricane liked men straightforward like her daddy. Heavy was glad she had no interest in him for his own personal reasons.

Breeze opens his eyes yet again to a blue, purple, and green, battered body still there.

Craig asked, "Taz what you going to do?" Breeze shook his head this is wrong.

Hurricane comes to but she did not want to make them aware that she awakens. She just wants to know who helped. If she lives, they all will pay. She is shocked once she realizes Breeze is there.

Hurricane knew it is him because she could see his shoe. No matter what kind of shoe he wore, he always had

Alicia Howard Presents

"Breeze" stitched on the front tip of his.
shoes.

The thought of him helping hurt her
and makes her sick. She talked with him
a week ago; he spoke on how he could
not wait for her to cook Thanksgiving
dinner. Hurricane wanted to cry her tear
ducts were worn out.

She hears Craig talking Hurricane
knew why he was here. She prays...

*"Heavenly father thanks you for this
day you have made. I know you do not
put more than we can bare upon us. I
carry this burden placed upon me today. If
you see fit to spare my life forgive in*

advance for making those that bring harm to me regret the day, they were born." As Hurricane finishes her prayer, she hears Taz say, "I am not fucking up my shoes by walking in the woods. Kick the bitch down there." Hurricane's soul hurts.

Her daddy said a man that got a woman with eyes like hers is a cold muthafucka, ain't ever lied.

Craig laughs but the sound of a shotgun kills the bullshitting. Taz jumps into the car as Craig kicks her as if he were trying to score a field goal at the Super Bowl.

Hurricane's body went rolling downhill into the woods. She feels sticks cutting her skin as she rolls.

Breeze looks at her in disbelief wishing he had gone against the grain like Mark. Taz knows how he feels about Hurricane he could see the hurt on Breeze face. Taz gave no fucks the bitch had to go. She was in the way he gave her three years of marriage.

Taz real woman fed up the money is not keeping her happy anymore. Rashida wants the man, the lifestyle, and most of all the money. Taz yells at Breeze, "You coming or staying here to sightsee?" he asks.

The second shot from the shotgun goes off. Breeze jumps into the car knowing the shots were coming from a hunter that lives nearby. He silently prays he finds her.

Chapter 3

Rashida talks on the phone with her bestie Tanya. "Girl for real, we're getting married soon." She is getting a manicure and pedicure in her home. Rashida the chick that always wanted to be something she will never be classy. She the bitch you could put in expensive shit yet her presence makes it look cheap.

"Girl I can't deal I do not see how you could fall for this shit. Taz is not about to leave Hurricane for you. That hoe got money running through her veins. What the fuck you got?" Tanya loves Rashida but she needs to learn she a bitch at the bottom. Where she will remain until she uses her brain instead of that raggedy ass pussy of hers. Bitch thought she had gold down there.

"Bitch, don't hate on me cause my man balling. I can't help this good pussy got him wanting to wife a bitch. Hurricane got money but she ain't a freak like me. The bitch too classy to get down and nasty like I do. You have to fuck and suck yo man, not all that cute shit. I mean swallow the dick until you throw up." Rashida is sick like that.

She would do anything in the bedroom to keep a nigga. That is how she keeping Taz. Rashida found out that he

into bitch on bitch action. She paid

Tanya a G to fuck her Rashida would spit

and licking all in Tanya pussy and ass.

Taz be so turned on he would stand

over them spraying nut everywhere.

"Hating? Your man? Bitch please!

That nigga is not neither one of our man.

He belongs to Hurricane, boo boo.

Without her, his money is short, I hope

she does leave his ass and let you have

him. Then I can see if she likes bitches I'll

take her fuck Taz."

Tanya is a wild redbone that makes

you double take when she walks through

the doors of the lesbian strip club. Rainbow Cloud she looks just like Pinky the porn star.

Taz ran the club but Hurricane owned it. Her father opened it when she was fifteen. Heavy got the idea from the gay clubs that jumped in New York. The shit is a source of income and Tanya the star of it all.

"Hahaha bitch, you so crazy I do not know why I fuck with you. I never thought about that maybe I should offer her some of this glass I got." Rashida pats between her legs.

The Chinese woman doing her feet shook her head. If this heifer had not offered three thousand for a home visit a week, she would have never came.

Rashida looked over the fact t in so many words Tanya let her know she still fucking Taz. She caught them fucking in his side apartment. She was pissed but Tanya did not see why she was mad since he did not belong to her.

Rashida a sidepiece like her Tanya also told Rashida if it were not her. It would have been some other bitch anyway. Rashida did not like it she loved

Taz, but she put up a front as if she down with M.O.N. (Money Over Niggas.)

She rolls with the shit because she knew by having his sons she set for life.

"Bitch that girl is not going to put her mouth on you. Your pussy talked about in the streets so much, Taz don't even be claiming y'all kids." Tanya wrong but telling the truth.

"I spoke to him about that. Taz said if niggas cracking jokes saying the kids might be theirs. He's not about to make him or Hurricane look bad by claiming them. I respect that nigga do too much." Rashida sighs.

"Whatever bitch, I got to go. I'm getting pampered you fucking up my vibe." Rashida is mad.

Not because she been Taz fool for the last ten years. For allowing people to get over on her period Rashida could not wait for Taz to take this bitch out.

People will be licking the crack of her ass after Hurricane dead. Rashida plans to bend over and enjoy every minute. Especially Tanya since think she is all that.

The bitch her bestie but fucking Rashida man more than her these days. Tanya told her Taz pay her she in it for the money. She lying Tanya had fallen for Taz. He made her get rid of three babies. He could not add her to his life.

Rashida knew everything because he would tell her. Taz knows she stupid Rashida rolls with the shit.

Rashida stands four foot eleven, a hundred seventy-five pounds, caramel skin, and bad acne hidden by make-up. She is not ugly just had the dirty girl look even when she called herself dressed up. No matter how hard a hoe tries to hide the fact she is a hoe.

It comes to the surface leaving them looking dirty. Rashida wonders what is going on she calls Taz phone. He noticed on the third ring. "Hey lovey."

Taz loves Rashida because she has been down with him. No matter what Taz will never leave even though a part of him has fallen for Tanya. He could not leave Rashida for her.

"Is she dead yet?" Taz looks at the phone then throws it out the window. He could not believe the shit Rashida pulls sometimes. This is a prime example of why he thinks about getting rid of her ass.

Taz is half the distance away from the location he left Hurricane body. Now without a damn phone if an important

caller will hit up Craig or Breeze. They

knew them niggas are always with him.

Alicia Howard Presents

Chapter 4

A heartbroken Breeze sits in the front seat with Taz. He feels like less than a man for going along with this. He wanted to warn her but could not bring himself to do it. Breeze knew if he mumbled a word Taz would kill him and his grandmother.

Taz hinted around to it when he brought this job to him, Craig, and the other people involve. Mark is the only person that did not fall in line. He told Taz he was out of his fucking mind. Taz tried to talk reckless to him, asking did he want to fuck her and shit like that.

Mark real name Marcus is a different breed of dude. He got his woman and her kids the fuck out of town.

Taz sent men to touch the man he was long gone. Breeze was there when Taz got the call on Mark he yelled *"Lucky bastard."*

Hurricane was also at the house when the call came wondering what is going on. Taz informed her that Mark had skipped town. Hurricane didn't understand Mark running off with money but she took Taz word for it.

Taz looks at Breeze he knows the nigga is bugging. Taz begin to pick his brain to see if he were the next person, he would have to kill. "Breeze, you ready to hit VIP tonight nigga?"

Craig jumps in. "I'm damn sure ready to toast to my new fucking position". He pats Taz on the shoulder as job well done.

"Man shut the fuck up, I'm talking to Breeze." Taz looks at Breeze.

"I'm going to lay low we all should for real. When do you plan to call in the missing person report?" Breeze asks.

"I got to wait seventy-two hours. We got to keeping moving like nothing happened, you feel me?" Taz wanted to know that Breeze is with him.

"Alright I'm down. I said I am in here I am!" Breeze knew the nigga is checking his resume.

"That's what the fuck I am talking about. y'all my rounds, got to have a few real niggas down with you." Taz is happy for now his team strong.

"You know we got yo back, dawg." Craig's dick riding ass wanted to climb the ladder of this lifestyle. He did not care who he cross to get there not even Taz. He just needs to learn a little more before trying to take him out the game.

Chapter 5

Wesley is out in the woods hunting as always. He from the Bronx made a good living for himself hustling in the streets. He is straight for the rest of his life. Wesley decided to get out the game.

His team nor his connect is happy about what he decided to do with his life. After telling them, he left state or so they thought. Wesley moved along the outskirts of NY.

He knew if he stayed the only way out was jail or hell. It is something about a hustler's mentality he did not understand. Most came into the business young due to hunger pains, cold nights

sleeping on a park bench, or running

from a broken family with no money and

nowhere to go.

What bothers him is once they were

in the game they make this a career.

Wesley been planning, saving, and

dreaming about the day he walks away

from this street shit. He invested money

in CDs, stocks, and bonds. Once Wesley

got the amount of money needed, he

invested in Microsoft stock. Now he is

thirty years old on chill mode.

Wesley is missing a few pages from

his book called life. However, he is no

longer looking over his shoulder for guns'
shots fired at him. Nor wondering whom
he could trust, or if bitches loved him or
the money.

The only bullets fired out here are
by hunters. Wesley joined the sport. It is
pretty dope for such a focus task. Wesley
sees something rolling down the hill
followed by the few shots he fired. He was
excited in six months of hunting this
would be his first prey.

"*Somebody's going to be eating deer
meat for weeks,*" he said to himself as he
walks over to the prey.

Alicia Howard Presents

The closer he got he thought his eyes were playing tricks on him. This is not a deer it's a person. Wesley ran to the body thinking *"Oh shit I done fucking shot someone."*

Wesley falls to his knees next to the body. The sight of it caused him to jump back. As it rolls on its back, he could tell it was a woman. Wesley wants to cry she looks like the night of the living dead.

He knew she was dead until he got close enough to see her chest rising and fall. Wesley does not know what she is fighting for she a helluva woman.

Alicia Howard Presents

Something told him not to call the police it more to this story. As he picks her up Wesley prays she lives to tell him who would do such a thing like this to her. Even though she is battered when Wesley picks her up, he could tell she has the body of a goddess.

This woman in beautiful the way her face looks at this moment. she may need surgery to get that beauty back. Wesley carries her inside.

Hurricane is in so much pain. When the stranger picked her up, she wanted to fight him for helping her. She wishes he had left her there to die. Then he took her

into a house with lights that caused
Hurricane to shake badly. She found the
strength to bury her head into his chest.
Hurricane wishes at this moment she was
married to him instead of the bastard
that did this.

Hurricane had been in the dark for
the past three days. Taz was trying to
make her give up the connects
information. He needs the plug to the city
after he tortured her. She gave it to him
knowing once he called it would throw up
a red flag.

The Mexicans don't fuck with
anyone but Hurricane and her father in

the last twenty years. Heavy was killed by

a bitch that wanted him to wife her. It

was one of their normal fights. Hurricane

was twenty years old when this happen.

Her father's funeral turned out to be

a double one because she had the bitch

touched so fast she buried them together.

Wesley laid her on the bed, she felt

like she had died and gone to heaven.

The bed is warm like heated seats in a

car. She doesn't know who this person is

Hurricane's is thankful for him. She

prays she lives to repay him. Wesley

could see tears roll down each one of her

cheeks. Her eyes were barely opens. He

didn't want Hurricane to think he would hurt her.

He kneels at the side of the bed in the guest room. "I hope you can hear me. I am not going to hurt you I want to help you as much as I can. If you don't trust me, give me a sign and I will call the ambulance to take you to the nearest hospital." Wesley wants to comfort her.

Hurricane did not move he was about to call the police. Wesley did not want this on his hands. Hurricane grabs his hand whispers, "Noooo". Tears roll because it painful to speak.

Alicia Howard Presents

Hurricane mouth is busted also missing teeth from Taz punching her in the face when she tried to fight back.

Chapter 6

"I am sorry I didn't mean to make you cry." Wesley is heartbroken watching this woman.

Hurricane shakes her head letting him know it's not his fault. He nods letting her know he understands how she feels. "I have a doctor coming here to look you over if you don't mind. I will pay for it, no matter what she says you need." e

Wesley knew this is a pay it forward moment considering how God has covered his ass so many times. Now he has a chance to do something for someone else.

"Please." Hurricane wants to stay low key. If she lived through this, she did not want to been seen. She wants to be felt from here on out.

"I got you ma, just rest here I'll be right back." Wesley walks out the room to get the phone. He dials the doctor heading back towards the room. There is a bathroom attached to this guestroom the tub with jet streams. Which is what Hurricane needs.

The water ran caused the mirror to become steamy. "Hello," the female voice says.

Alicia Howard Presents

Wesley forgot that he called Trinity. She is a doctor at the local hospital. "Hey baby, I need you to come by my house as soon as you can love." She smiles.

"What didn't I do for this nightcap?" Trinity has not been with him in a while. The man gave her fever six feet five, two-hundred-fifty pounds of sexy Mocha chocolate, body hard as a brick, and dick for days.

She has been missing him, he told her he is not looking for a woman like her. Trinity is too busy for him Wesley needs someone flexible like him. Those can move when they want to.

Trinity understood that, and asked if sex is out. He agreed to the sex if she did not get crazy on him. So far, things are good, she is hoping all the freaky moves she pulling in the bedroom would give him a change of heart.

"No baby, that's not what I'm on right now. I have some serious shit going on here. I can't speak on it over this phone when can you come?" He looks over at Hurricane.

"I am scrubbing in for surgery soon as it's done, I am leaving. I'm on call tonight instead of a set time." Trinity said that because times that she is on call Wesley would sex her in between calls.

On the lucky nights she never was called in, he would sex her all night. Trinity hopes tonight is the night.

"Great, I will be here call me when you need to be buzzed in." Wesley's house is in the cut with a private entrance.

"Ok boo, I got you. Do you need anything?" She asks this all the time because he is one of the few that needs nothing.

"Yes, bring all the medical stuff you can love." Wesley shocked her by saying yes. His request is even stranger to her.

Trinity did not know what he had gotten into but she would find out sooner than later.

"I will do my best", she assures him.

"Thanks," he replies before hanging up the phone.

Hurricane could hear him talking to the doctor. She likes that he is honest, and not hiding anything from her. It makes her feel safe now. Wesley walks back into the bedroom sitting on the bed this time. "Can you try to walk if I help you?" he asks her.

Hurricane did not know where he is taking her. Yet she trusts him enough to find out. Therefore, she nods her head yes. Wesley smiles at her. She did not need to see all the way to tell he fine.

She wonders, *"Why in the hell she had to meet a man like him right after she had gotten her ass whooped."* She chuckles a little Wesley sees it.

"What could possibly be funny to you He asks. She shakes her from side-to-side indicating nothing.

This caused Wesley to smile again. "I am going to grab your legs to turn you sideways. Then lift you up with each hand," he told her.

Hurricane shakes her head letting him know she understands what is taking place. Wesley did as he said once she was on her feet the room begin to spin and her body sways. Wesley caught her places one of her arms around his waist. As he places one of his arms around Hurricane.

"When I move, you move." He stepped Hurricane stepped with him. As he sings Ludacris *"When I Move You Move."* She is delighted. Hurricane doesn't know who this crazy man is but she will always love him for this.

Hurricane took all the strength she had in her body to nudge him. He is making her laugh on the inside and causing her pain on the outside. She thinks one of her ribs is broken.

"Okay, damn I'm sorry no partying." Wesley got her to the bathroom fast with all the aches and pain by acting silly.

He sat her on a chaise. "I need to take off your clothing to put you in the tub." Wesley did not want to do anything without informing her. As he scoops up some hot water pouring it over Hurricane's hands. The feeling caused her to close her eyes and moan.

"Hmmmmm." She needs to feel that water

all over her.

Chapter 7

"Can I?" he asks.

"Please." Hurricane begs the strange man to put her in the tub. They say it is a first for everything this damn sure is a first.

Wesley helped her get undressed, and then into the tub. It is burning the hell out of Hurricane due to open wounds. Epsom salt and lavender is in the water to help her with aches and pains.

She rests her head lying back on the plush neck pillow Wesley gave her. As he rinses the dried up blood off her body, the water quickly turns red. He got her

out the tub, cleaned it, and refilled it

before placing her back in to soak.

Hurricane was in awe with this

man. He is very respectful, not once

trying to feel her up, which is shocking.

Once Wesley got her settled in the

tub, he dims the lights and lit a few

stress relief candles from Bath and Body

Works. He had found her some pajamas

and a dry towel to have when she wanted

to get out. "Okay miss, you're all clean

now, but relax long as you like. If you

need me call, I will hear you. The

intercom is on. No matter what room I am

in, even outside I will hear you." Wesley

says before walking out.

"Hurricane," she says.

"Excuse me?" Wesley stopped.

"I'm Hurricane," she says again.

He smiles. "That's a helluva name

now I understand your strength." Wesley

went to leave.

"Please stay!" Hurricane is begging

again with no shame.

Wesley sat on the chaise next to the

tub that facing the door. He did not want

to stare at her body. He had been fighting

his manhood this whole time. "I'm here

Hurricane, I'm here." After hearing, she doses off to sleep.

Wesley got her out, dressed her, and then put her to bed. Hurricane slept the whole time like a newborn baby.

He looks at her, dimming the bedroom light as he walks out. "Goodnight Hurricane."

She was not sleep; she was enjoying the pampering he gives. "Goodnight stranger." He never heard her.

Chapter 8

Taz's head is banging. VIP was live last night. There where bitches everywhere, ass and pussy popping, and titties shaking all up in the place. For a minute, Taz thought he was up in the Rainbow Cloud.

Taz had a fucking ball. The only thing that got in his way all night was Rashida. She had to come out with him, which Taz normally did not allow. He did not want to chance being caught by Hurricane.

Hurricane never knew Rashida was Taz woman or the mother of his children.

Rashida nor any other bitch had balls big enough to step to Hurricane with some silly shit. Taz laughs thinking about the fact she was a boss in every way.

He never loved Hurricane, he wants what she had to offer. Taz put a plan in motion to get it from the day he met her. Hurricane thought the greed had just set in, but this has been Taz's plan from the gate.

"Hmmm." Rashida is laid up in Hurricane's bed as if she is the queen. Taz looks at her smiling. He loves Rashida she a gutter, ride or die bitch for Taz.

it did not matter how many women he fucks. He is fucking her best friend Rashida knew it she did not care. All she could see is them as a power couple. That hustles bitches together by any means necessary.

Taz knows the shit with Tanya is getting out of hand. He plans to fuck her a few more times than he would have Rashida fire her at some point. Taz did not want to be around her anymore. Nor is he going to allow her to tear his family apart.

Alicia Howard Presents

Rashida has been loyal and understanding all these years. Now it's her time to be treated like a queen.

"Did you sleep well?" Taz asks her. The bed Rashida has at home is nothing like this one. Hurricane bed is custom-made Baldacchino Supreme Bed.

This is the most expensive bed available on the market. Its hand carved by Stuart Hughes and made from three types of wood namely Ash, Cherry, and Classy Canopy. The interior of the bed is accessorizing by twenty-four carat gold. That weighs over two hundred pounds.

Alicia Howard Presents

There are only two Baldacchino Supremes' ever created, and one belongs to Hurricane.

"Yes daddy, I did. I can't believe how amazing this bed is." Rashida rolls around in it feeling like she is on vacation. Since her boys were with her mom. This would soon be Rashida fulltime lifestyle.

"Baby can you make breakfast before you go?" Taz is hungry but more so spoil. Hurricane is a street bitch but she knew how to take care of her man. Her father taught her to do all the things her mother did for him to win his heart over.

Every morning Hurricane sucks his dick, fed him breakfast in bed, fucks him, ran a hot bath, and once Taz is out she oils his body, and help dress him. Hurricane missed doing this a few times due to business.

"Cook? Ewe No! I do not cook babe. Ain't a maid up in this big bitch?" Rashida says speaking of Hurricane home. She did not understand why the heifer needs this much space. Hurricane did not even have children.

Alicia Howard Presents

The mansion sits on Chestnut Hill Drive in upper Brookville, NY. It has a private gate entry that leads to a magnificent estate with seven bedrooms. Nine bathrooms, and four half baths it also features a stunning mahogany library and grand piano spaces.

The lower level is fully equipped with a bowling alley, gym, and movie theatre. An indoor and outdoor pool and tennis court.

Hurricane didn't allow outside help in the home. She said that her father taught her *"The same bitch you bring in to help cook and clean your home will be the same bitch that helps fuck your man."* Taz

felt her on that cause let her had hired a

bitch, he would have been fucking her

every chance he got.

"Well we about to change that. We

are going to hire some help around here

once I move up in here. That is what is

wrong with these hoes. So scare of being

cheated on. That shit dead! Ain't no nigga

cheating when he knows you will fuck

that bitch right along with him." Rashida

says as if she is speaking straight

knowledge.

"I hear you baby. I guess I will eat cereal. Fuck! I can't." Taz shakes his head.

Rashida is sitting up in the bed now "Why not?" She loves cereal.

Hurricane didn't allow cereal in the house. she said it's not real food." Taz is confused. He had not done shit for himself in so long he did not know what to do.

"Oh nooo! Ugh, I hate uppity ass bitches. They make me so damn sick. I know you glad that bitch is dead." Rashida see why he never fell in love with the bitch. Hurricane was too anal.

"Yeah I am." He did not know if he is telling the truth but it sounds good.

"Get dressed; we'll go out to eat." Rashida hops out the bed.

"Cool. I need to eat before I contact the police about my missing wife." Taz says he is standing there looking crazy. Rashida did not know what is wrong with him.

"What's the matter?" she asks.

"I don't know where my clothing at." Taz is lost.

"Are you fucking serious? Did the bitch bathe you, too?" Rashida's mind is blown.

He is ashamed to answer. "Yes," he replies holding his head down.

"Hell naw! I will not be doing all that extra shit. I do not even bathe my kids. They do their own shit, okay. I don't know what to tell you." She washes her pussy in the bathroom sink. When Taz saw her do this he was about to die.

"You can't do that! Hurricane..." the look Rashida gave him let him know that Hurricane is no longer here. From the looks, a lot of shit is about to change.

The first thing is Taz would have to learn to take care of himself. He joins Rashida as she washes her pussy in the sink. He washed his dick in the sink it didn't feel good.

Rashida used the good towel to dry in between her legs. Taz did the same, but he looks around as if he thought Hurricane would catch him. When Rashida put back on her clothing from last night, he figured he would do the same cause he did not know where shit was.

Hurricane had spoiled him to the max. Taz suddenly thought that he had not thought this plan out well.

Chapter 9

Craig is on his bullshit when he walks in the breakfast spot on Lenox Avenue. He had gotten a call from Taz asking him to meet him for breakfast. Craig did not understand why they were eating out this morning.

Since they were, he did not drop the two bad bitches he has with him off. He walks into the place as if he is ten feet tall with a bitch on each arm. This nigga put you in the mind of Craig Mack the rapper, but dark skinned.

He is so glad he would be the face of the street he did not know how to act.

Alicia Howard Presents

Taz watches him come in. Rashida smiles because she loves to see a nigga on his pimp shit. Her father had made hoes running in and out of their house. Her mother did not mind one bit. Hell, he had kids by Rashida mother and the mom sister. She used to tell Rashida. *"A man is going to cheat whether you approve or not. So make it easy on him by letting him bring his bitches home or yo ass going to have many of nights sleeping alone."*

One of the hoes killed Rashida father. she wanted to get out the business. Rashida father was not feeling that. He whoops her ass sent her back to the tracks to make money.

She was waiting for him to pick up the money. The moment he walked through her door. she put six bullets from a .45 in his ass.

Sadie didn't run she waited for the police. She sits in jail right now today. Yet she would rather live in a cell than walk the tracks for him ever again. Rashida's mother was lost without him. She used drugs until she overdosed leaving Rashida all alone with no one, not even siblings.

Alicia Howard Presents

"So you're a pimp now?" Taz asks as he watches the excitement dance around in Rashida's eyes. She loved that life Rashida use to get down for him until they came up on Hurricane.

Part of Taz thinks she still trick on the side just for the hell.

"No, these are just two friend of mine, Stacy and Tammy." The women spoke as they had a seat.

"Good, cause with what we got going on there is no time for a petty hustle like pimping." Taz nibbles at his bacon. Rashida did not like that statement. Unlike Hurricane, Rashida did not understood that women are supposed to be seen not heard.

"That ain't no muthafuckin petty hustle. My father took care of his families well, boo." Rashida is out of pocket.

"Bitch you grew up in the projects and both of your parents dead, am I correct?" Taz hates to embarrass her but she has to learn when and when not to speak.

"Yes, your correct daddy." Rashida holds her head down thinks about the reason her father's pimp game never taken seriously by other pimps or his hoes. Rashida mother was always out of pocket.

Taz looks back at Craig. "I need you to drop these hoes off. find Breeze, and kick it with him for a while. Pick his brain because I need to know what he thinking. I will be making the call today they won't put out an alert until tomorrow which is the seventy-two-hour mark." He needs Craig to be focus because they were not home free yet.

"I'm on it boss." The women did not like to be address the way Taz just done. Nothing is coming in way of them getting the money. They said their goodbyes just as fast as they said hello.

Taz orders Rashida to go home and stay there until further notice. He did not need her in his face or asking stupid question around the police.

Nor did he want them questioning who she is. He knew this shit would take time so there is no need to get her hopes up high.

Alicia Howard Presents

Chapter 10

The buzz went throughout the house scaring the hell out of Hurricane. She jumps out the bed wondering where in the hell she is. Her body is weak causing her to fall to the floor. She cries.

"Daddy why are you not here to help me? Why did I think he loved me? How did I let him run game on me? I am Hurricane how dare he." She lays on the floor of the strange room crying.

Wesley jumps out of his bed. He is wondering who in the hell it could it be this time of morning. As he glances out the window the sun sneaks out of the clouds. He hops out of bed hitting the intercom. "Who is it?" his voice booms raspy from sleep.

"It's me boo." Trinity chimes.

"Trinity?" For a moment, he wonders why she is there. She knew what he is thinking since she can't stop by unannounced.

"Yeah, you told me to come by and to bring all my medical stuff." Trinity says refreshing his memory.

"I sure did." Wesley buzzed the gate to let her in. It's about five a.m. Maria is up and moving by now. "Maria." She walks in carrying the portable intercom because she hates yelling.

"Si?" she replies. Wesley laughed cause as always she is up working by three a.m., and in bed by five p.m., He loves this woman.

"Let Dr. Dagwood in," Wesley states.

"Hmmmm, si", she mumbles doing as she is told.

"Thank you." Wesley knew she did not care for Trinity. He did not know why she disliked her, but it's something.

Wesley made his way to the room Hurricane is occupying. When Wesley opens the door, he finds Hurricane on the floor. He rushes inside.

"Babe... I mean Hurricane, are you okay?" Wesley could see the tears on her face. He did not know if they were due to the pain in her body or heart.

She cries more. "How could he? How could he? Everything my father worked for to pass down to me when he died. Even his title in the streets I gave this bitch ass nigga everything my father taught me a man needs.

I am Hurricane. I am the Queen. How could he?" she cries. Now that Wesley has the small version, of how all this happened to her. He damn sure wants to hear the long version. First, he must get her well. Wesley was about to speak when he heard Maria's voice come through the intercom.

"Mr. Charleston, your guest is here. Should I seat her or send her up?" she asks as if she had never met Trinity. Trinity rolls her eyes behind Maria's head. She did not know why the old bitch had it out for her. If she has her way, the bitch will be the first thing she removes from Wesley's life.

"Send her up please". He responds. Hurricane thinks, "*Why is the rich black man helping her"*. She knows soon as she is well she going to shake him.

Hurricane would die before she let Taz live off her daddy's hard work. Hurricane assumes this square helping her now is a good place to heal.

"Of course we are coming up sir. what wing are you in?" Maria climbs the steps knowing Trinity hates them, she prefers elevator.

"Forgive me the west wing." Wesley says directing them to him.

Wesley is on the floor holding Hurricane in his arms when Maria and Trinity walk in. Maria smile as Trinity gasped for air. Hurricane saw the look on Trinity's face. Whomever she is, was not gasping at her battered face. She is gasping at the fact her man was holding another woman.

"Look ma'am, I'm not trying to take your man." Hurricane tries to lift herself up but couldn't. Wesley and Maria help her stand. "I will be getting my stuff and going." Hurricane informs the woman who looks relived after hearing that.

"This is not my lady she my friend the doctor. Yo ass not going anywhere hell, you can't even walk." Wesley says as Hurricane leans on Maria.

Alicia Howard Presents

"No dear, you must rest you're not well pretty girl, si." Maria smiles at her. Hurricane likes this old Spanish woman because if she looked anything like she felt she is not pretty.

"Maria, help me get her back in bed so Dr. Dagwood can examine her." Trinity watches them rave over this stranger.

The friendship statement did not hurt her; she is hurt to see the love he has for this women. Trinity knows she has to be someone from his past.

"No I am not his woman; we are great friends. If everyone will leave the room, I can examine you from head to

toe." Trinity plays nice for the moment.

Maria walked out the room. "Mami,

if you need me just call si?" She says.

Hurricane smiles nodding her head,

"Si". She guesses house cleaners were not

what her dad made them out to be.

"Hurricane, I will be right outside

the door if you need me." Wesley gently

released her hand.

"I'm sure she will be just fine."

Trinity could not wait to speak with him.

He walks out the room as if he were

leaving his wife. It's something about the

woman that gave him butterflies, in a

good way. Something he has not felt since high school.

He wants to help her even though something told him she did not need his help.

Trinity is a doctor of all trades holding a few titles in the medical field. She is an OB/MD doctor and chief of executive at the hospital. Baby girl is eating well but the demands of the career made her personal life hell.

Trinity walks over to the bed. "I'm going to start with a woman examine if you don't mind. Is there anything I should know before I start?" she asks

Hurricane.

Chapter 11

"I was a few weeks pregnant but I know that's over with now. I have been raped by five different men less than twenty-four hours ago." Hurricane let her tears fall freely.

"I am sorry to hear this. Do you know who would do such a thing to you?" Trinity asks as she gathers the things she need to examine her.

"Yes I do." Hurricane looks her dead in the eye.

"We should call the law then get you to a hospital." Trinity could already tell the injuries she had would not kill her.

Hurricane has survived through the night. the hospital would suggest admitting her which means getting her away from Wesley.

"I am the law; I just need to get well. Do not worry I will not be here long. I will send for my driver as soon as I can walk." Hurricane told her.

Trinity looks at the battered woman thinking *"Driver? Yeah okay, and I am Michelle Obama."* However, her mouth says, "That sounds great honey, now let me see what I can do for you." She put on a fake smile.

Hurricane knows she does not believe her. She is not in the mood to prove shit to a simple bitch. That is in love with a man that does not want her. Hurricane lays there as she being examine.

Hurricane knows she has been shot in the hip and lower back. The rest of the shit would check out as minor shit. All she could think about is how she would kill Taz and every nigga that helped him.

Taz thinks she is dumb but Hurricane knows about the bitch Rashida. As long as the bitch stayed in her lane, she was good. Now that they think she is dead, that will be his main woman for sure.

Trinity found that the baby is no longer there. She cleans Hurricane out. The rest will discard her during her normal cycle. It should come within a few days due to the miscarriage. The damage they done may cause her never to have children,

Trinity hates to tell Hurricane the news because she knows firsthand how the thought of never being a mother feels. Hurricane also has broken ribs. She wraps Hurricane with an ace bandage in due time they would heal.

She sedated her to remove the two bullets still in her body. Trinity could do nothing for the bruising to her face or body. Some scars will heal while others might cause for cosmetic surgery.

By the time, Trinity finish Hurricane is sound asleep. She does not know this woman's life. Trinity knows she does not want it. She walked out the room hoping this is the first, and last time she will see Hurricane in this house again.

Wesley almost knocked Trinity down as she came out the room." Is she going to be okay?" He is worried. Trinity had been in the room for a few hours.

"She will be fine they did a number on her. She says she knows who did this. Hurricane doesn't want to bring the law in because she is the law. Whatever that means." Trinity chuckled she is not a street chick so she did not understand what Hurricane said to her. However, Wesley does.

"I'm glad she's cool." He walks down the steps.

"How do you know her?" Trinity is curious she knows Wesley is from the streets. She thought that life was behind him now.

"I *don't* know her I was hunting her body came rolling down the hill. I thought she was a fucking deer. Once I realized it was woman I bring her in and called you. I didn't know how long you would be so I bathe her then put her to bed", Wesley informs her.

"That's a fucking stranger up there? Are you crazy? You don't know if people are still looking for her." Trinity could not believe her ears.

"They left her for dead that happens in the streets T. What you want me to do, leave her outside?" Wesley is getting pissed. This is part of the reason does not have a woman. He does not have time for the bullshit.

"Call the damn police like a normal person." Trinity is disgusted with him.

"Once I found out if she was okay, I asked her if she wanted me to call the police and she begged me not to. so I called you because I understand her not wanting the involved. I am from the streets too." Wesley reminds her.

"I thought you were above the streets now?" Trinity asks him.

"I am not above anything rich people think they are above shit. I am out the game but I will always respect it. Because it made me the man I am today." Wesley waves his hand around to show what he has accomplished.

"I get that!" Trinity says.

"No you don't! You never worked for anything. You were given everything." Wesley pulls her card. Trinity told him how her father is the Dean at Harvard. Her mother is a lawyer with a private practice. She knows nothing about earning her keep.

"I guess I don't! It is not my fault I was born into money. what's up with all the friend comment?" Trinity is pissed now.

"It's not me or Hurricane's fault we were born in the hood either. Trinity, we have always been friends that have sex sometime." Wesley reminds her.

"I see." Trinity is hurt.

"I need a nap send me an invoice for the service. Give Maria the scripts she needs so she can pick them up." Wesley walks away from her.

"Maria, can you see Dr. Dagwood out?"

"Gladly." Maria says.

Chapter 12

"I am calling to make a police report." Taz doesn't realize how calm he sounds.

"Sir, is someone hurt, or missing?" the dispatcher asks.

"yes, my wife has been missing for three days now," Taz says as if he really doesn't care.

"Sir, is this common for her? Did she take her car? Did she leave with someone?" she asks.

"No this is not like her!" He tries to sound worried. "She has never gone this long unless it's a business trip. My wife always informs me when she is leaving town. Yes, she left in her car a few days ago. I call the night she didn't return home. However, I was informed she must be missing for seventy hours or more. Do you people understand what can take place in that amount of time?" Taz asks her.

Breeze and Craig had come by this morning to take her car to park it near the place they left her body. so it would look abandon. "Sir, I am sorry to hear this is taking place. We do understand what can happen in this time frame. It the law we don't make the rules here. we will need you to come down to this office.

Please bring in your photo ID, any

personal information you have such as

weight, height, skin, color, and age.

Anything else you have that you feel

that might be helpful would be great. if

she was having an affair a potential love

name and number would be great," she

assures him.

Taz couldn't believe the nervous of

the bitch talking about an affair. "I will be

there in a few hours," Taz says to her.

"Ugh, okay see you then," She

doesn't trust the bastard on the opposite

end of the phone. He doesn't seem

unhappy, or hurt his wife has been

missing for days. Also he is in no rush to

bring the information needed down there.

as she thought on his action this is

going in her red flag file. just in case

bullshit came in to play later on down the

line.

Taz hangs up with her smiles as he

looked at the ringing phone. He had to

get the dispatcher off the phone this is

the second time Pablo has called.

Pablo Jr is the middle that handle

thing between Hurricane, and his father.

His father Pablo Sr., is the person that

talked Hurricane father into moving to

New York. This lifelong friend was making

them so much money in the Chi. he knew

they would make a large profit in the N.Y.

Heavy would still be alive if he would

have listened. Pablo Sr. would say to him

"My friend, you will never find one like

you had (*speaking of Hurricane's mother*),

so just get you a Spanish woman to make

you happy my friend." Heavy didn't listen.

Pablo Sr. has never been the same

since that bitch killed his friend. Pablo

Jr., semi took over about five years after

the death of Hurricane's father. Pablo Sr.,

felt it was time for him to rest. he was in

the background make sure thing ran smoothly.

Taz picks up the phone. "What a surprise." He has given Pablo his number many of times. when he would meet with Hurricane. Taz would ask him to plug him so he could put the nigga he know down south on. The nigga would always say *"Someday my friend."* leaving Taz in his feelings.

"Where is Hurricane? She has a shipment coming in. I have been calling her phone for days, no answers, no answer my friend!" Pablo is sweet on Hurricane, but he doesn't care too much for Taz. He respects him because he is her husband. Yet he knows her father is rolling over in his grave behind her marrying this clown.

Pablo is tall for a Mexican... six foot even, two hundred pounds with oh my god abs, sun-kiss skin, Caesar haircut and a goatee. He doesn't understand how she got with a lame like Taz.

"She's not here man I can get the shipment if you tell me where to pick it up." Taz doesn't know where the product is dropped off nor picked up. he only knows where the street distributions warehouse location Hurricane has is.

Whenever they were there, the product came in by carrier. Hurricane is serious about her business. Taz would tell her *"I should know this thing just in case something happens to you."*

Her response was *"Once I am dead, you are out the business."* She knows that Pablo wouldn't never do business with him. Pablo Jr told her this on her wedding day his father agreed. They didn't think Taz was certified enough to handle this business, and all its glory.

"That's not the way we do business, my friend. It's a man's job to know where his wife is at all times." Pablo doesn't

know what is going on but something
doesn't feel right.

"I will make sure she gets your
message," Taz is pissed by the statement
made about not knowing where his wife
is.

"No! make sure she calls me ASAP."
Pablo hangs up.

Taz wants to throw the damn phone
across the room. he couldn't because this
is his business phone. That nigga Pablo
is going to have to see him one day for
trying to play him like a little loc. He
could call Hurricane's phone all the hell

he wants; she isn't going to answer because the bitch is dead.

Now is his time to be the man with or without Pablo. However, Taz couldn't focus on that now; he has to get down to the police station to make the missing person's report. As he is walking out the door, Craig calls.

"Speak." Taz was in a shitty mood the evident is in his voice.

"The car..." Craig was about to say too much.

"Thank you. I got to go handle something I will get with you later." Taz hangs up the phone pulls out the

driveway heading to the police station to
file the report.

CHAPTER 13

Pablo has the funniest feeling he just can't shake. He jumps on the phone to make a call. "Carlos,"

"Hey Pablo," the Mexican loved to hear this man voice because it meant money.

"Don't send my sister to visit yet," he says.

"Why? She is ready to go!" Carlos doesn't like the sound of this. Pablo's family has never had an issue as this.

"I have to run out of town for a corporate matter and I can't have her out here unaccompanied. If I misplaced her that would kill both us," Pablo educated him.

"I comprehend but I don't think mum will be pleased," Carlos says speaking of his superior.

"I know this woman won't but I will make it up to her," he guaranteed him.

"I am certain you will," Carlos told him.

"Give me a few days," Pablo informed him.

"I will adjust her flight today," Carlos jumps off the phone because the merchandise was being weighed down to go out. Conditions has triggered Pablo to put an interruption on the delivery Carlos knows that something severe has occurred.

Pablo's father doesn't know anything is happening. Once he strides in on the conversation hearing his son putting a suspension on the shipment. Pablo Sr. hasn't received anything from the streets, so he curious about whatever reason he made a demand like this.

When his son turns around to leave the headquarters. He finds his father standing close by. "How much did you overhear?" Pablo knows his father well.

"Enough questioning what would make you do such a thing," Pablo Sr. says.

"Hurricane hasn't been taking my calls for a few days. She has never done this, and wouldn't do it this close to shipment," Pablo Jr. s.

"Is she okay? Have you spoke to her husband?" The inquiries he questioned made Pablo Sr. nauseate to his stomach. He knows that his colleague/trade partner would have never permitted this marriage to happen.

"I did but he is a fool. He doesn't know where she's is, also told me to send the shipment to him. He needs to know where the carrier is to pick it up. Hurricane haven't shared the location with him. I told him to have her call ASAP. Hurricane hasn't called yet - I am still waiting," Pablo Jr. doesn't like the feel of this.

"Hurricane is fine, just hold tight. You already made a boss move to suspense the shipment. You don't want the product in the wrong muthafucka hands. I am proud of you for handling this.

Nevertheless, I can see you're letting emotions get involved in this." Pablo Jr tries to speak his father stops him.

"Don't! Hurricane isn't your woman or wife let thing play themselves out." Pablo Sr know his son is ready to head over to Hurricane house, but that isn't his place.

"Thank you Papa, that means a lot to me. I want to run this business just as you do. I know Hurricane handles business just like her father did. That's why none of this makes sense to me," Pablo Jr is stressing.

"Stay out of it, son," this father knows his son well.

"Terminado," Pablo Jr. says as he sits down in the office chair.

"Promise me. You're all I got! Please don't make an old man come into a war zone, cause for mines I will," Pablo Sr. is a very dangerous man.

"Prometo," Pablo Jr sighs because once he gave his father his word he has to stand on it.

"I love you, son," Pablo Sr. walks out the office.

"Love you too, Papa." Pablo Jr says.

CHAPTER 14

"Thank you again for lunch Ms. Maria." This woman has been treating Hurricane so well. She could definitely get used to this treatment. Hurricane doesn't know what her daddy was thinking, but this maid shit isn't half-bad.

"No it's just Maria, pretty," Maria smiles at her.

"Ok Maria. I'll stop adding miscalling you miss, if you stop calling me pretty, it's Hurricane," she told her. Maria gave her a mirror to look at her face. It wasn't as bad as the bruising on her body and soul.

"Okay, okay, Hurricane - you got a deal." Wesley is standing at the door unnoticed smiling. As he watches the two interact, he has never seen Maria treat anyone this nice. Hell, not even him and she has been with him for ten years now.

"I see you all are having fun, but Hurricane it's time for your meds." Wesley says. He has been giving them to her so she wouldn't have much pain. She is even making it to the bathroom on her own. Hurricane is a very strong woman considering what she has been through. "Mr. Charleston I am leaving. I have laundry to fold," Maria said Kissing

Alicia Howard Presents

Hurricane on the cheek. Maria likes
Hurricane because she looks like her
daughter Selena. She passed six years
ago in a car accident. Selena was Maria
only child.

Maria sat in the hospital with
Selena until she died. Her daughter,
was bruised up as Hurricane as
current state, yet their beauty still
spills through.

"Wow, I don't get one?" Wesley
teased. "You're my favorite boy - of
course," She kisses his cheek and
he laughs as she pops him across
the butt on her way out. "She is a

great lady. I wish I could take her with me," Hurricane informs him.

"She's sweet but not cheap," Wesley, laughs.

"That's even better cause I'm rich," Hurricane assures him.

Wesley looks at her, to see if Hurricane is joking but she isn't.

"Is that right?" Wesley asked even though he doesn't believe her.

"I'm not who you think I am," Hurricane pulled the cover over her as he sits on the bed beside her.

Alicia Howard Presents

"Who are you?" Wesley wants to know all that she willing to share about herself.

"My name is Heather Douglas; my father is Heavy; I mean...."

"Heavy's your father?" Wesley cut her off. He knows Heavy well; hell, half the shit he has is because of Heavy. Wesley never knew that he had a daughter because he never spoke of her. He only spoken of his wife's passing a short while after he made it to New York. At the time Wesley was a lil' dude trying to learn the game.

"Yup," Hurricane shakes her head. If she spoke right now she would cry. She missed Heavy so much, that is the reason she married Taz so fast. Hurricane felt like she was in this world alone.

Heavy always told her that street bitches don't need love. He said the shit so often that she has it tattooed on right hip. Hurricane lived by that until he was killed. Now she understands what he meant because love is more of a want than a need.

You would die if you don't have it. Yet people act as if they can't live without it. Sometimes the shit you are dying to have will be the same shit that damn near kills you.

CHAPTER 15

Wesley heard about Heavy's death. Though he left the hood, he still has friends he touches bases with to get the word on the streets. It's funny because no one ever told him she took over for her father's business. Wesley could remember when Heavy asked him to work for him.

Wesley said to him "No".

Heavy asks, "Why not?" It wasn't because he was into forcing niggas to work for him. Heavy was just curious why he would turn down the money.

Wesley responded, "I don't want to work for you. I want to have my own just like you," he was fifteen.

Heavy laughs at him. "If you find five runners that will work for you, I will help you do just that," Ever since then Wesley's been getting money.

He remembers that conversation like it was yesterday. Hurricane looks as if she is about to cry, Wesley slid in bed beside Hurricane to hold her. "I'm sorry for your loss," he says to her.

Wesley empathized with Hurricane but couldn't have sympathy for her.

Alicia Howard Presents

Wesley never knew his parents. He was found in the dumpster left for dead.

Mrs. Walker found him one night when she was taking out her trash. Mrs. Walker kept him until he left on his own at fourteen. Mrs. Walker wasn't a bad lady she was a drunk that told him too often *"I should have left you in the dumpster."* He couldn't live with that negativity; it isn't good for a man's soul.

Hurricane lies in his arms. "Thank you. I just wish he was here. I thought I found someone to love me. It turns out that doesn't. He had to be plotting on me from the day we met. I treated that man as if he were a fucking god, as my father taught me.

"This is the thanks I get. The fucking thanks I get!" Hurricane went from hurt to mad as hell. She is a street bitch if Taz truly think he will get away with this He got serious mental issues.

"Can I ask how you met this man?" Wesley is curious.

"I went to the club the weekend after my father died, with a friend of mines. We were in VIP. I only went to clear my head. Taz was watching me from across the room. As I sit at a table full of women. He was popping bottles, dressed from head to toe in Gucci. He is five feet eight, deep

brown skin with two gold teeth at the

bottom on the fangs. I remember thinking

he look good. I think I was horny Anyway

we were leaving he stepped to me and

asking for my number.

I ask did he have a car and he told

me yeah. I told him I wanted to ride with

him because I didn't want to go home

alone. That nigga had a Rolls Royce and

even took me to his Penthouse. It was

nice and all but when you're used to shit

like that you're not impressed.

I was just glad to meet a man

getting as much money as I was. He kept

that act up for about three months then the lies unfolded. The house was his homeboy's, the fucking car was rented and past due. They had been looking for the thing he had was hiding it.

I should have left him where I fucking found him. No I was in love or needed love, I kept the lame ass nigga. I even ended up buy him a Rolls Royce he drives right now 'til this day. Damn. I was stupid wasn't I?" Hurricane looks at Wesley's face for the first time.

She jumps back when she realized that he has four gold teeth - Two at the top and two on the bottom fangs.

"Why are you jumping? Oh, the fangs?" Wesley chuckles. "I'm nothing like that bitch ass nigga. You can let that idea exit your brain. I got my own shit." Wesley looks around the guest room.

"To answer your question, no you weren't stupid; you were hurting and looking for something to fill that void. Instead of being a man loving on you as he should, he plotted against you," Wesley looked her in the eyes causing Hurricane to feel naked.

"Ouch!" A pain hit her in the side. She had forgotten to take the meds.

"Damn my fault, I forgot to give you your meds." Wesley hands her the pills and bottled water he had place on the nightstand when he came in.

Hurricane drank them down quickly before saying, "Thank you."

Wesley gets up. "I better let you get some rest, and don't worry about rushing to leave. You're welcome to stay here as long as you like," Wesley told her.

"I'm leaving as soon as I can make it down the steps. I don't want to have to fuck your doctor girlfriend up," Wesley loves Hurricane gangsta. Wesley isn't

getting all of it yet. She keeps spilling it
bit by bit.

"Trinity is not my girlfriend. I am not
looking for a girlfriend. I want a woman.
At the moment you can't fuck up anyone.
That lil doctor girl be done kicked your
ass," Wesley says while laughing.

Hurricane throws a pillow at him.
"Hey, that's fucked up." She laughs until
the pain kicked in.

"Ouch," Hurricane grabs her side.

"Too early?" Wesley ask.

"Never too early to joke around!"
Hurricane laughs. As she silently thanks
God this man has found her.

Alicia Howard Presents

"I'm going to bed now," Wesley says
before getting ready to exit the room.

"Aye, do you want to watch a movie
with me? I'm not sleepy," Hurricane ask
him.

"Cool, but I get to pick. I'm not
watching no bitch flick." Wesley joins her
in bed.

"Nigga, I don't watch bitch flicks. I
like it gangsta or action. I'm a street
bitch!" Hurricane reminds him.

"Yes you are," They watched
Scarface until they both fell asleep.

CHAPTER 16

Taz is in the back of the Rainbow Cloud counting money the club brought it in this week. Seventy-five thousand isn't bad. He also collected Hurricane money from the streets. Taz plans to find a plug. He knows that Pablo wouldn't fuck with him.

Once this shit hit the airwaves tomorrow that Hurricane is missing.

Taz is angry with himself because he never broke Hurricane to the point she gave him information he needed like access to her bank account or safe deposit box in the house. He isn't stressing because once the dead body and abandon car is found they have to release all her shit to him, anyway.

Taz will have it made, if he could get Pablo Jr to keep fucking with him. He knows that won't happen. Cuban business deals usually have a long line of history behind it. That's why their asses didn't get caught or locked up as much as niggas do. They are very careful whom they break bread with.

Tanya came off the stage from doing her number. She heads to the office to turn in her money. Yet that isn't her only reason for going to the office. Taz has been acting funny since he pulled this shit on Hurricane. Tanya loves him but she thought it was fucked up. Hurricane is a solid bitch. Even though she is fucking the bitch's man, she has respect for Hurricane.

It was about the money for Tanya at first. Once Rashida told her how Taz is planning to set Hurricane up, Tanya decides she make him hers. Tanya is a bad bitch but she holds no candle to Hurricane or what she bought to the table.

When she found out that Rashida is the one holding his heart. Tanya knows taking him would be like stealing candy from a baby. She knocks on the door before entering. Hurricane never allowed people to bust up in her office. In all the time Tanya has work there, only one girl tried it.

Hurricane shot the bitch in the chest when she came through the door, called the police as the bitch died. Hurricane didn't do one day in jail. She claims she thought a robbery was about to take place. The cops let her walk with that shit.

Alicia Howard Presents

"Who is it?" Taz is putting the money in the office safe it's the only safe he has the code too.

"Me, daddy," Tanya whines.

"Me who?'" He knows damn well it's Tanya. She is the only one that called him daddy. Rashida would when he talked to her like a pimp.

"Tanya nigga," She is pissed with his actions lately.

"Come in," Taz says as he sits down at the desk.

Tanya walks in wearing an all-black crotch less suit. All her outfits are crotch less. She enjoys the nasty hoe that didn't know her from a can of paint. However, sucks her pussy on while she is on stage. "Hey daddy"

Tanya is sexy as fuck. He knows it's time to end this shit. Taz has enough on his plate. He refuses to add Tanya drama to it. "You got my percentage?" Taz asks her.

"Oh, so that's how we jamming now?" Tanya leans on the desk. She couldn't believe that his lame ass is trying to play her.

"I am married baby; you know what this is." Taz doesn't know that she knows what has taken place.

"Really? Where is Hurricane?" Tanya ask him. Taz could tell by the tone of her voice she knows something.

"What?" Taz wonders what she knows.

"You heard me that bitch Rashida tells me everything. I know what you did. I can't believe you that type of nigga. I still love yo stupid ass. I know I could never replace Hurricane. Now that she's dead, you and I both know Rashida is no match for me," Tanya walks around the desk standing between Taz legs. She took his hand and placed it on her shaved pussy.

Taz finger instantly dips in and out of her. The bitch has that kind of magic on him. Whenever he is near her pussy he gets weak. "Tanya we are done. Rashida has history and kids on you," Taz schools her while playing in her pussy, juices running down his hand.

Tanya rides his fingers as if they are a dick. "Hmmmm, okay daddy. Just make me come one last time, please....ooooh please." Her moans drive the nigga wild. Taz dick is so hard he grabs Tanya, throw her on top of the desk. Yanks his pants down roughly entering her. "Yes, yes, yess, gotdamn yes." Tanya smile inwardly. She knows he loves her pussy.

"Oh, fuck this shit hard, pleeeeeaaase," Tanya yells knowing that he is about to cum. He never lasted over ten minutes with her. However, each time those ten minutes were the best of her life.

"Bitch shut up, I'm cumming!" Taz know that he could cum inside of Tanya because she would get an abortion at the drop of a dime if he told her to. Hell, she doesn't want kids anyway.

He lays on top of Tanya huffing. "It's really over this time."

Alicia Howard Presents

"I love you," Tanya informs him.

"I love you too." Taz dick is still inside of her hardening again. He is down for round two.

CHAPTER 17

"I can't believe him," Michelle says.

"I know girl this shit is burning me up." Michelle listens to her best friend Trinity. She is angry about the things that Wesley is doing. Michelle doesn't care Wesley is fucking up. She knew he would fuck up. Trinity wants to see the change in him. Once a street nigga always a street nigga.

"I don't know why you want him, anyway. You only met him when he banged himself up riding that motor bike thingy," Michelle is disgusted with the whole situation.

"I know. I fell for his swag and charm that day even though, he told me he wasn't looking for a woman. I just knew after a few times of me letting out my inner freak. Wesley would fall madly in love with me," Trinity is crying now.

"Nooo sweetie, don't cry guys like that are jerks. They don't know how to love because they've been hurt so much in their life. He just wants to use you to patch this hood rat up. Wesley is stupid if he's not thinking about her drama coming to his door.

Well maybe he's got one of those glock thingy's there," Michelle hates thugs. That's why she is a government attorney that helps throw as many in jail as she could. Michelle is supposed to help the ones that she could but she doesn't. It's not her fault they were born in the gutter.

"You say Wesley doesn't know how to love but he loves on her. Even the damn house cleaner loves this bitch. I can't let her have him, I just can't." Trinity needs Wesley in her life. She is sick of the squares from the family country club her father keeps trying to hook her up with. She wants an ambitious, strong, sexy man with amazing dick.

"Honey, Wesley loves her because they're both trash. You need to call Ballas Truman, and take him up on his offer. He is the man for you; seven figures, big feet..."

Trinity cut her off "Yes huge feet with a dick the size of a peanut. I tried to fuck that man and couldn't feel shit until Ballas was about cum his nasty ass stuck his dick in my booty cheeks filling it up with cum," Trinity shivers reliving the moment.

Alicia Howard Presents

"I never knew that god he is gross."

Michelle couldn't image such a thing. She

thanks God for her husband Walter

Herman III. There is no man in the world

like him. She met in college when Walter

was pre-med like Trinity.

They all went to Princeton where

Michelle took up law. She knew that she

would marry money. Michelle would not

play herself. It didn't hurt that Walter is

fine as hell. He is light skinned, brown

hair with natural honey blonde

highlights, five feet seven, with a stocky

football build. Walter was on the varsity

football team and it didn't hurt that his family is well known in the community.

Trinity had a good man in college - Webster Solomon. His family is rolling in cash. Trinity parent were crazy about him; he was studying to be an entertainment lawyer. She dated him all four years and was engaged to him.

Trinity called it off a few months before the wedding. Saying she didn't love him her mother was pissed. She told Trinity, "You don't marry for love; stability is the key love will follow later," Trinity wasn't feeling that. She wants to be head over hills in love.

"I never wanted to share that with anyone. It's not like that's a highlight of my life." Trinity has no highlights of her life outside of this job of hers. Trinity is pushing thirty-five, still no kids or husband.

This is shameful to her mother because she couldn't brag about grandchildren like the rest of her friends. Trinity often ignores her mother's calls because she doesn't want to deal with the bullshit.

"You can share anything with me, you know I love you and want see you happy," Michelle assured her.

"Thanks girl, you're the best," Trinity told her.

"Oh girl I have to go Walter is here; he's bringing a co-worker home for dinner. I will see if he's single," Michele hangs up.

Trinity looks at the phone laughing at her bestie trying to be a matchmaker.

CHAPTER 18

Maria cooks breakfast she feels it's time for Hurricane to eat real food. Hurricane can't get out that bed if she doesn't have the strength. Maria cooked biscuits, grits, eggs, beef bacon, and toast with mimosa. She knows that little kick in the orange juice would get Hurricane going.

Hurricane has almost been here a week now, and Maria wants to help her walk freely. As Maria places the food on the trays to take to the room. She watches the television as a familiar face came across the screen. The reporter says, *"We have breaking news. I want to report a missing woman. That was last seen a week days ago leaving her house to go shopping."* When Maria saw Hurricane's face she ran up the stairs bursting in the room to find Hurricane and Wesley in the same bed asleep. She turned the television on to the news.

"Wake up, wake up," Maria yells.

as she turns the televisions to the new reporter is going on. *"This woman was last seen driving a pink Bentley. Wearing a black fur, pink shirt, black jeans, and pink quarter length booties all designer. We have her husband here with us he will give us a little more detail." The*

reporter hands the mic to Taz.

"I am Tazaves Blackmon. My wife,

Heather Douglas- Blackmon has not been

home in a week. This is not like Heather at

all. I know something is not right. I can

feel it. I need my wife back; she is

everything to me.

I don't understand how people do

things like this. Heather is known as

Hurricane to her friends and family.

Please bring her back to me." Taz acts as

if he is broken down.

The nerve of this bastard!

Hurricane couldn't believe her fucking

eyes. The reporter jumps back in. *"This is a sad moment for the Blackmon family. If you have any information, please call 555-555-3245 or visit our website for photos of Heather.*

As well as additional information on her. Mr. Blackmon is also offering a five-thousand-dollar reward if she is found dead or alive. More details on that is available on the website as well. Back to your normal programming."

The television pops back to the talk show Maria had been watching. She doesn't know what is going on. Maria looks at Hurricane who has tears streaming down her face. Wesley looks at

Maria she knew they need a minute to

talk. Maria walks out the room but not

before kissing Hurricane's cheek and

saying "What doesn't kill you will make

you stronger," After those words, Maria

leaves.

Wesley waits for Hurricane to speak.

"The nerve of this bastard to file a fucking

missing person's report. As if he doesn't

know what the fuck happened to me. The

bitch is banking on me being deceased.

Taz even got a fucking price on my head!

What kind of shit is this Wesley? How can

a person take your hand in marriage vow

to love you, try to kill you?" Hurricane got

out the bed walking to the bathroom.

Hurricane is in pain but she would

have to deal with it. She can't let this shit

ride. Wesley watches her then says, "I

don't know what kind of nigga moves like

that. I know one thing, your father

wouldn't lay down for this and if..." she

cut him off.

"If what?" Hurricane wipes herself

and hand. Then came out the bathroom.

"If you think I am laying down for this

you're out of your muthafuckin mind. I

have never laid down for shit in my life. I

won't start today Taz fucked up by not

putting a bullet in my head. When he kicked me down the hill, and left me for dead. I need something to put on and a ride to the city, resting time is over." Hurricane enlightens Wesley.

"I will get you a jogging suit with a hood. It might be a little big on you." Wesley ran out the room to retrieve the clothing Hurricane needs. What she doesn't know yet is that Wesley isn't dropping her off alone; anywhere Hurricane going he is going with her.

Hurricane paces the floor thinking about all the niggas she had played, fucked, dogged out, and used for money she didn't even need. Hurricane wonders

if this karma. Does she deserve this shit

Taz has thrown her way?

Hurricane sits down on the bed

when a pain hit her. As soon as the pain

passes, her shipment came to mind. She

jumps off the bed running to the bedroom

door. "Wesley!" He was coming in the

room. When Hurricane runs dead into his

hard body. It knocks the wind out of her

a little because she is moving too fast.

"What's the matter?" Wesley grabs

her by the waist. Holding Hurricane close

to him. She lays her head on his chest to

let another pain pass.

Alicia Howard Presents

Once she caught her breathe "I need to make a phone call," Hurricane whispers. The broken ribs are slowing her down. That is the only pain she couldn't deal with. Wesley knows the pain is kicking Hurricane ass, but know he can't convince her to stay put.

Wesley carries her to the bed. "I know you got shit to do but take your time babe. Your body is not healed yet be easy don't overdo it." He hands her his cell phone. Hurricane dials Pablo's number. Wesley walks into the bathroom in Hurricane room to get dress.

CHAPTER 19

Pablo Jr. is sitting in the den with his father smoking a cigar, sipping cognac when the news report came on with the story about Hurricane. He damn near drops his drink on the Italian rug.

"Papai, do you see this shit? Is this clown for fucking real? Even if this is true why would he handle things this way? This move is for an average bitch, not Hurricane.

Then a five-thousand-dollar reward for her? The person that finds her fucking car can get more than he offered for her body," Pablo Sr. watches his son carry on about the madness spilling from the television.

He looks to an angle that is hand painted on the on the ceiling of the room.

"Heavy, I fucked up. I didn't take care of your baby girl as I promised. I allowed her to marry this nothing ass nigga. When I know I should have stopped it, but I didn't feel it is my place.

Yet it was I am the only familia she has. My son is head over heels in love with her even though she can't see it. I don't think she will ever see the love Pablo Jr. has for her, which is probably for the best.

Business and pleasures is never good. That is the main reason your daughter's face is on the news because of mixing business with pleasure. However, something tells me, my friend that she is not there with you.

Nevertheless, if she is, whoever has the balls to do this with the life of his or her familia. That is my word. Te amo mi amigo," Pablo Sr. is about to say something when the servant came in.

"Excuse me, sorry to bother you Mr. Escobar but you have a call." He hands him the cell phone. The Escobar's never answers calls directly his servant or driver does.

"Who is it?" Pablo Jr. asks.

"They wouldn't say, they demand to speak with you immediately," He knows his boss wouldn't like that.

"Gracias, Roberto." That is his queue to exit the room. Pablo Jr doesn't get many unexpected calls. He wondering who would call his phone demanding anything.

Pablo Jr. holds the phone to his ear but doesn't speak. He listening to the background noise Pablo Jr got nothing until the voice chimes in. "Don't freak out. I am hurt but I am not dead. That bastard along with a few of his friends put a hurting on me. Nothing that can't heal or plastic surgery won't fix," Hurricane assures him.

"Thank God. I just saw this on the news. I didn't know how I am going to make it without you in my life." Pablo Jr. smile is so bright it caused his father to chuckle.

"You would have made it out just fine. Everybody wants to work for you," Hurricane informs him. Pablo Jr isn't thinking about money.

"You're right about that but I only do business with la familia," Pablo Jr. reminds her. That's part of the reason she takes none of his advance as flirting because they we are familia.

"Indeed we only trust la familia. Did your sister flight come in yet?" Hurricane needs to know.

"No, I canceled her trip once I couldn't find you." Pablo Jr, assures Hurricane the shipment is safe.

"I am sure mama is upset." Hurricane wonders about the supplier.

"Yes. I heard she would be but I promised to make it up to her." Pablo Jr.

informed her of his promise to double up on the next shipment.

"Indeed, she will have a longer stay." Hurricane agrees stating fact it would take longer to move the work.

"Hmmm, time will fly watch." Pablo Jr doesn't think it would be too hard.

"Of course tell Pablo, Sr., I am going to handle this my way, not his," Hurricane know her father's friend well. He would have Taz touched before she makes it to the city if she doesn't stop him.

Pablo Jr looks at his father. "I will tell him," His father shakes his head. The girl is too much like her father. This is her war he will stand down, but he ready when she needs him.

"Thanks. I will call you when I am settled." Hurricane hangs up.

Hurricane jumps into the jogging suit that Wesley left on the bed. She is glad that her product is safe. Now it's time to put together a game plan, to get back everything that has been taken from her.

"When will you have enough money to quit?" Wesley asks. He is dress in a jogging suit identical to hers, just a different shade of gray.

"I already do," Hurricane makes up the bed she has been in for the first time in week.

"So why are you still do it?" Wesley isn't judging her; he just wants to understand her.

"This is a family business. I will die doing this. Once I am gone my children will take over. That's just the way things are," Hurricane informs him.

"I understand," Wesley wants her to know that he is on her side.

"Why are you dress?" Hurricane ask.

"I'm coming with you," Wesley told her.

"This isn't your war. I'm a big girl, I will be fine just drop me off," Hurricane says.

"Okay babe, let's go," Wesley walks out the room as she follows him.

CHAPTER 20

Trinity is sitting in her office sipping coffee when the news airs Hurricane's missing person report. She damn near spilled her drink trying to get a pen to write the contact number down. Trinity couldn't believe that Hurricane has a husband looking for her.

While she is laid up in Wesley's house. Trinity doesn't understand how a woman could not call her husband. This is such a selfish act she picks up the phone and dials Wesley.

He is sitting in the car outside of Bank of Manhattan when the phone rings. Hurricane just walked inside.

Wesley see Trinity's name come across

the screen. He starts not to answer it, but

he knows that she will keep calling.

"Hello,"

"Wesley," Trinity says.

"Trinity don't start with that

bullshit," he is sick of her uppity ways.

That is the reason he can't fuck with her.

Wesley won't deal with her family or

friends frowning their noses down at him.

Everything he has is earned by hustling

and hard work. No one will make him feel

ashamed of that.

"Where is Hurricane, I mean Heather?" Trinity asks.

When she said Hurricane's government name Wesley knew the bitch has seen the report. "Trinity why?"

"Well her husband is looking for her. Has she called him yet? I started to call myself. That poor man must love his wife to go this far," Trinity states but could care less how much he loves his wife.

Trinity is glad to know that the bitch will be away from her man soon. She had Wesley right where she wanted him. Then this gutter bucket hoe shows up beaten and battered, taking her shine.

"Trinity you need to mind your own fucking business. Don't get in this shit or you will find yourself dead. It's not a game. You don't understand how people move in these streets. The same man that was on the news today confessing his love is the same muthafucka that left her for dead." Wesley is pissed. This bitch has lost her mind.

"Why would he do a thing like that to his own wife? If he did, she must be some kind of monster. I don't know why you would want her either," Trinity thought Hurricane was making it up. That her husband did this to her. She has never heard such foolishness in all her life. These type of things only happens on television.

"Hurricane a fucking street bitch, Hurricane is the queen of the streets! She runs the streets all the way from Harlem back to Manhattan. The nigga wants her spot that's the only reason he married her. This news shit it just a stunt to cover his ass.

You are too damn absent minded to understand shit like that. Not everyone grew up in a fancy house, house cleaners, and expensive cars. Some of us have to grind, hustle, and take what the fuck we want." Wesley is so outdone with this bitch. He knows that Trinity is uppity, but damn she an airhead, too?

"Well Heather shouldn't be doing that with her life anyway. I am glad that you are no longer that person." Trinity praises Wesley hoping she is right.

"Trinity baby, I will always be that person. I don't play in traffic nor shit where I eat, but my hand still holds all the cards my dear. How the hell do you think I afford my lifestyle?" Wesley schools her ass fast.

Yes, it is true Wesley isn't active in the game but he will forever collect money from these streets. That is something he plans to teach Trinity how to do once all this shit is behind her.

"Oh my God, you can't be serious? Wesley stop being greedy, you don't need the money," Trinity wants to cry. This bitch has come in awakened a monster.

"It's not that easy love; you don't clock in or out for this shit. You live it, die in it, or go to jail. Those are the only real outs no matter how far you move away the game is here to stay," Wesley know people that live closer to him now. That get higher than the best junkie out from the hood does.

Once he found that out, he put his people on his game. Never allowing one dime slip away; you could ball today and be homeless tomorrow.

"Wesley, I don't know who you are!" Trinity is somewhat scared and turned on by him right now.

"You never took the time to find out," Wesley said before hanging up.

Trinity won't let him get away like that. She picks up the phone dialing the number from the news. The dispatcher picks up. "Missing Person Alert, how may I help you?" she asks.

"I want to speak with someone on the case of Heather Douglas-Blackmon," Trinity has to get rid of this bitch.

"Just one moment," The dispatcher transfers her call.

Hurricane is in the office with one of the bankers. She never does a transaction out in the open today isn't different. Hurricane dealt with the same person every time she comes. Nicole is not only her bank manager but also her friend.

Over the years of doing business with this bank, they have gotten close. Hurricane is wearing a light grey hoodie jogging suit with, a black pea coat, and shades. Nicole knows the line of work Hurricane in she her on the news.

Nicole is a white girl from the suburbs, yet she could see Taz's bullshit a mile away. It's funny she has never met him. Hurricane comes to the bank alone.

As she enters the office with the things Hurricane asks for. Nicole sits down at the desk across from Hurricane.

"Bitch, I got the pre-paid visa loaded with ten grand, ten grand in cash, and a fake driver's license," Nicole runs the list down she requests on the ride over.

"Thanks bitch! You're all I got besides them crazy ass Escobar's," Hurricane smiles.

"I'm here for you, boo," They stand up Nicole hugs her. Nicole has grown to love this crazy street bitch. Nicole kids loves themselves some aunt Hurricane.

Hurricane gives the best gifts.

"I can't believe all this is happening

to me. I thought he loved me the nigga

tried to kill me. Now he files a missing

person report to cover his tracks. Taz is

hoping someone will find my dead body.

So he can shine off the shit my daddy

built," Hurricane is cries.

"Girl wipe ya muthafuckin eyes. You

know niggas ain't shit; look at my kid's

daddies not helping a bitch out." Nicole

leans in whispering, "That's why I linked

up with a bitch like you. Also catch that

fine ass DA too, stop all that crying. Make

that nigga wish his daddy never busts in his mama's pussy," Hurricane laughs. Nicole is to hip because of too much black dick.

"I can't with your ass, I'm gone; you haven't seen me," Hurricane told her.

"I am legally blind and I can barely see," Nicole jokes around.

"Too much Facebook heifer," Hurricane walks out laughing.

Hurricane remembers the video Nicole mimic's dropped a week before her life changed. She walks out the back ready for war. Wesley wants to embark on this journey with her but she can't allow that. Hurricane doesn't know what he

has come into her life. Whatever the

reason is Hurricane won't be able to find

out, until all of this is behind her.

CHAPTER 21

They pulled up to the Waldorf Astoria Hotel. Nicole set everything up for her just asked. She needs to clear her head so she can put a plan in motion.

That's not going to be easy to do with Wesley around. Nicole even had a car being dropped off for her later today. Hurricane wants to be near her house but not too close.

As she tries to get out of the car Wesley grabs her wrist. "Hold on let me park," He is not leaving her alone.

"No Wesley! I hope this is not the last time I will see you. I need to do this alone." Hurricane hands him the envelope with the ten thousand cash in it. "This ain't much but I had to give you something for the love you and Maria showed me." She holds the envelop out to him.

"Girl you better you get that shit the fuck up out my face. I found you in my yard, I can't leave you here. I asked you if you want the cops involved. You told me no I respected that but don't fucking insult me. By throwing that little ass money in my face." Wesley could eye ball how much is in there.

"I don't know what you want from me. I got too much shit on my plate that I need to handle. Go back to the hide out you were in these streets are not for everyone.

I learned that when I found a nigga like you hiding in the woods. I don't know what made you want to hide from the streets, but I don't want to hide. I want my muthafuckin spot back," Hurricane yells at him.

"You're an ungrateful bitch. Get the fuck out my car Hurricane. I care about your ass for some dumb ass reason. But it's cool do you here's a tip. . You're dead;

act like a ghost and touch whoever hurt you. Hopefully this doesn't fuck you out of ever having a man to love you for real." Wesley pissed.

Hurricane don't know shit about him to say anything about his life. Nor where he lives or why he is there.

"Fuck you Wesley! I never ask for your help." Hurricane jumps out the car.

Who does he think he is? How can he care for her when he doesn't even know her? A nigga that she's been with for years tried to kill her. Now this nigga thinks she is about to trust a nigga she has only known a few days.

"No you didn't ask for it but you damn sure needed it." Wesley drove off.

If Hurricane wants to be alone that is fine by him. Wesley doesn't have time to play captain save a hoe anyway.

Rashida finds the news report funny as hell. She picks up the phone calling Tanya. "Girl did you see that nigga acting like he really cares about that bitch? Girl Taz stupid. I wish he would have given that bitch car to me. Shit I would have pushed that pretty bitch around." She laughs as she puffs the weed.

"Girl he couldn't give you that damn car. Taz had to make it look like she was car jacked and shit." Tanya thought this hoe has to be the dumbest bitch on the planet.

Tanya can't wait until she talks Taz into dropping the bitch. Rashida isn't going to be a good look for his image.

"I guess, but I am going to have Taz buy me one just like it once all this shit is over." Rashida has been dreaming of the day she could shine like this. She is so glad it's finally coming true.

"Girl, fuck a car! Your ass better be putting some of that money away. You see what he just did to Hurricane. How you know that he won't do the same shit to your ass? Girl I would be watching my back with that nigga at all times." Tanya is putting on; she is just trying to get in

Rashida's head cause problems between her and Taz.

"That muthafucka know not to try me. I'm a hood bitch! I wish that nigga would. I'm not going to lay down like that hoe. If that was me, we both would have died believe that." Rashida was is talking mad shit but she knows that she didn't have shit for Taz to kill her for. She might kill his ass if he tries to drop her after this shit is over.

"I know that shit's right, that's why I fucks with you. Hurricane is a street bitch on that money side but we hood bitches. We don't give a fuck who we got to cross to get what we want. You feel me?" Tanya know that Rashida isn't reading between the lines on what she is saying.

"That's right girl let me get off this phone. I'm going shopping since that's the only thing Taz allows me to do right now. I can't even party or shit. Let me go before that ten o'clock curfew kick in," Rashida is sick of shopping.

That shit doesn't move her like that anymore. Rashida is ready to be sitting in VIP acting like *that bitch.*

"Bitch, get me something," Tanya told her. She is dead ass serious. Rashida

Alicia Howard Presents

has bought most of the clothing she

owned in the last few years.

CHAPTER 22

Taz is hanging out with Breeze and Craig. He found out the other three niggas that helped him torture Hurricane skipped town on his ass. After he gave them the money he promised them.

"Man I can't stand a pussy ass nigga." Taz is mad because the niggas could name him if they ever got jammed up.

"I know! That's some bitch ass shit," Craig says.

"Right! It's fucked up but it is what it is, ain't no need to be sweating the small shit," Breeze says coming to terms with what he has done. It's no turning back now. He has many friends questioning him about the issue. Breeze acts as if he doesn't know shit.

"This shit is going to be water under the fucking bridge soon. I need you to make that call about the car location," Taz told Craig.

"Man I handled that already," Craig assures him. That's what Taz likes to hear people getting shit done.

"Is Pablo Jr. going to get in bed with us on getting this money?" Breeze asks.

"That nigga acting like a bitch! The last time he called talking about he can only talk to Hurricane. The shipment was due to come in he stopped it. Pablo Jr. hasn't called since this shit has aired on the news." Taz hates that nigga.

"Damn," Breeze know they need that plug without it, all of this was pointless. He didn't do this shit for Taz to eat off the money Hurricane has tucked away. This was a major come up for him. That little twenty G's that Taz gave them isn't shit. That's why he doesn't understand why those fools ran off. Breeze wants the full reward for this shit.

Craig was about to speak when Taz's phone rang. He smiles when he sees the news report's number come across the phone. Craig smiles because he knows once they find the car they will search within fifty miles of the surrounding area for the body.

Once Hurricane body is found dead, they will be in the clear and shit could go as planned. Craig bet that bitch wish he was her nigga now instead of Taz. He wouldn't have done her dirty like this nigga did.

"I have a tip for you," The person over the case told him. Taz just know she is about to say she found the car.

"I am listening; please tell me you found my wife." Taz plays the concern husband role.

"I'm not sure, this lady left a number for you to call her directly. Also we have a lead on the car. It's where it is reported to be. It's totaled, but it's in the vicinity that the lady called from about your wife," she told him.

Taz is shock wondering what this woman knows about his wife other than she is dead. Taz is sick to his stomach. "Thank you, I will call the number now," Taz assures her.

"If you find her we want the exclusive interview with her," she told him.

"Of course," Taz wants to yell "*Bitch how you going to get an interview from a dead woman.*" However, he plays it cool dialing the number given to him.

Trinity doesn't identify the number when it came across the screen. She picks up "Dr. Dagwood's office,"

Taz looks at the phone wondering did he have the right number. "I was given this number by missing persons. I'm sorry if I have the wrong number," Taz says hoping he does.

"Oh no, you're Hurricane's I mean Heathers husband. I know you must be worried sick about her, but she is fine. I treated her myself," Trinity says.

Taz almost dropped the damn phone. "What? Are you serious? Where is she?" Taz couldn't believe this bitch is still alive. After all she has been through.

"She is at my friend Wesley Charleston's house." Trinity gave him the address so Taz could send the law to get his wife. Once Hurricane is gone, she could slowly work her magic on Wesley again to make him fall in love with her for good this time.

Wesley doesn't need a no woman that would lie on her husband. It's obvious she has since this man is happy that she is still alive.

"Thank you so much ma' am. I don't know how to repay you," Taz says faking the joy.

"Helping you find your wife is thanks enough for me," Trinity told him. She is glad he was coming to get his got damn wife; she is in the way.

Trinity knows that Wesley told her to stay out of it, but everything isn't as street or hood as he thinks it is.

Craig and Breeze stares at Taz while he looks as if he is about to have a heart attack. They don't know who he is on the phone with but they could tell it isn't good from the look on his face.

"What the fuck is up man?" Craig asks. He really doesn't care what it is because he doesn't plan to do any jail time. Behind this shit no matter who he has to dime out.

"This doctor bitch says she treated Hurricane. She is alive and well staying at some friend of hers house name Wesley Charleston," Taz says.

Breeze got him a chair to sit on cause the nigga seem like he is about to pass out.

"WC? I know that nigga we went to school together. We use to clown the nigga about how he is hood with a rich white boy name. I guess that's where he went to hide out after he killed the three niggas that killed his cousin.

That nigga is a heavy player in the game. I think he still got a hand in it and not on a low level. If she's with him you're not going to be able to run up in that joint. You gotta at least let the cops find out if she's there," Craig schools him.

Taz know that is going to be fucked up for them if Hurricane is there and remembers who did this to her.

"Man I am not prepared for this bitch living through this. I should have put one in her head, damn," Taz says, as if Hurricane was just a nigga on the street.

"We need to lay on that bitch that gave up the information. Have the house she gave us checked out. If she's lying, we're going to get rid of her ass. As of now we're the only ones that know that she is claiming that Hurricane is alive," Breeze is right if the shit does or doesn't check out. The bitch has to go before she get to running her mouth.

"Now you're thinking my nigga. I was worried about you, but you coming around acting like a real team player in this shit. I appreciate that, for real son." Taz is back on his feet now.

He got on the phone calling the missing person alert worker back to inform her of the information he has found out. She told him she would get someone over there to check things out ASAP and as soon as she heard something, she would call him back.

In the meantime, Breeze has track down a home location for Trinity Dagwood. They heading out to where she lived hating that the information she has is deadly.

CHAPTER 23

"Bitch ass nigga, give your cousin up," The nigga said as he had the gun to Twan's head.

"Muthafucka if you going to kill me you better do just that, bitch ass nigga." Whack! The second dude in the car sitting behind the first gunmen hit Twan in the head from the backseat. He winced in pain as blood leaked from his face.

"Muthafucka you're going to die out this bitch for another nigga," The third person in the car said. He was in the seat directly behind Twan.

"It's not just any nigga, that's my muthafuckin family. I watched that man earn every fuckin thing he got. You think I'm going to lay down and let y'all bitch ass niggas take it from him? Fuck that!

Kill me because blood is all the fuck you getting out of me." Twan loved WC and there was no way he was going to let the nigga rob him even if it cost him his life.

The driver in the front seat nodded his head. The nigga sitting directly behind Twan blew his head off. The nigga on the passenger side not only pushed Twan out of his own ride, but pulled off in his shit leaving Twan on the ground twitching.

Wesley jumps up out of his sleep. He could see the video the cops had retrieved from the gas station where his cousin was killed. Twan wasn't blood because Wesley doesn't know any of his blood relatives, but this was a nigga he been stomping with from kindergarten until the day he died.

When Wesley got that call, he was laying up in a bitch's house that Twan had put him on. She was hard to get Twan knew that if no one could break her, WC could. All Wesley had been thinking about after he fucked her was *I can't wait to tell cuz I bagged this bitch, and she super nasty too.* He chuckles when the thought came to his mind.

Wesley remembers going down to the police station to see the video. They wanted him to identify the men in the car. He could have but he didn't; they were Twan's runners that's how they gotten in his car.

Twan never saw it coming because he was good to these cats. That's the thing about this business no matter how nice you were. When a muthafucka wanted your spot they would kill you in cold blood to get it.

The police kept asking Wesley, *"Do you know these men? What do you have that they want him to give up?"* They knew it had something to do with drugs but they had nothing on Wesley that counted. He has never been caught dirty never been locked up for anything in his life.

When he walked out the precinct, he knew that he would kill them all. Then get the fuck out the game. He couldn't deal with niggas wanting to take shit from you verses muthafuckas getting up getting their own shit as him and Twan did.

That's why it pissed him off when Hurricane acting like he was is bitch ass nigga running from the game.
No, he was running from three murders he committed all on the same day.

Only reason there isn't a warrant for his arrest because they couldn't place him at the crime scene cause the time frame are so close, the men were killed five minutes apart. They felt it was impossible for him to pull that off alone.

Maria came in his room. "Mr. Charleston, the police are downstairs," she says walking out. When they tried to question her showing her Hurricane's picture. She acts as if she doesn't speak English. Then she came to get Wesley so he could handle things.

"What the fuck?" Wesley has never had the police come to his house since he has been living here. What the fuck could they want now? He hops out of bed with only pajama pants on heads down the steps without putting on a shirt. When Wesley sees a male and a female cop. He realizes that might not have been a good idea.

Alicia Howard Presents

The female cop has to blink her eyes a few times to get the dirty thoughts out of her mind. The hair going down his navel ran right into the V formation that led to his happy place is everything. "How are you gorgeous...? I mean sir." Wesley laughs as she almost dies.

She wants him to bite here with them fangs. Maria seen this woman embarrassing herself. She came handing Wesley a shirt, nodding her head for him to put it on.

He pulls the shirt over his head noticing the male cop staring at him strangely. "How may I help y'all?" Wesley asks wanting them to get the hell out of his house.

"Long time no see, WC," the male cop says. Wesley knew that he looks familiar. He is one of the cops from the murder of his cousin.

"Yeah, long time. Is that what brings y'all here today? Y'all got a lead on who killed my cousin?" Wesley asks knowing damn well that isn't the reason.

"No, these guys all were found dead. We are here about the young lady Heather Douglas Blackmon. We got a report that she is being cared for here," the cop says.

"I'm sorry to hear that happened to them guys. This Heather person I have never heard of her. I saw it on the news but I don't know why the tipper would lead you here. If it means anything to you, I am willing to let you look around but I can assure that no one beside and my maid reside here," Wesley told them.

The female cop asks, "Maybe she is someone you dating or a friend of your wife," she smiles at him.

"By the looks of that picture you all showed me I would have remembered dating that woman. She couldn't be a friend of my wife because I don't have one yet. As I said before, y'all are free to look

around," Wesley says waving his hand

around the house.

CHAPTER 24

The male cop has seen all he wants to see. These street niggas get to live in mansions he is barely affording the small hundred-thousand-dollar house he is living in. "No, we have seen enough. We will be in touch if we need further information," they said before walking out the door.

Wesley begins to think what would make them come to his home looking for Hurricane. Then the light came on Trinity.

Wesley yells, "Maria." She came to see what he needs.

"Get the realtor on the phone tell her I am ready to see that house she has been trying to get me to upgrade to." Wesley doesn't like heat coming down on him as it is now.

He made his way upstairs to call Trinity's phone. She didn't pick up; he knows that she often came home crashing most mornings. therefore, he knows that she is there. Wesley needs to warn her of the danger coming her way. He gets dressed as fast as he could then head over to her place.

Taz is getting his hair cut when the Missing Person Alert number came across his phone. "Mr. Blackmon speaking," he chimes in the phone.

"Yes, I am calling you to tell you the lead was a bust. I'm so sorry that we had you thinking that your wife was coming home. The officers went to the address and spoke to the homeowner. They didn't know her at all sorry again, Mr. Blackmon."

"It's not your fault thank you for all that you have done for me," Taz says her. The bitch claims she helped Hurricane. He doesn't care what she done for her. He wants to keep it as Hurricane is dead. As far as he is concern no one else has seen her but this woman. He would silence her ass before she goes public with this shit.

Taz hit Craig line he picks up. "Yeah boss."

"Take her out she lied," Taz says.

"I'm on it," Craig chucks her up to being some greedy bitch that wants the money. Breeze and him seen her come home from work in her scrubs an hour ago. They hopped out the work truck dress as electricians knocking on her door, waiting for Trinity to answer.

CHAPTER 25

Trinity is in the shower when she heard her phone ringing like crazy. She hopes that it isn't the damn hospital. Trinity isn't in the mood to double back. Her body needs rest all she wants to do is jump in her bed with the Kindle, and read a good book by Fanita Pendleton.

She has been overworking herself lately. Trinity is thinking about early retirement even though she knows her family wouldn't be happy about it. However, she is pushing forty with nothing to show for it but degrees and money.

Alicia Howard Presents

Trinity wants something more meaningful. She grew up around money, yet no one really seems happy about life.

As she steps out the shower, she takes her time to dry her body. She isn't in a rush to find out who had called her. Trinity needs some alone time. She walked into her bedroom to look for her phone. Once she spots it the doorbell rang.

From the way things are looking, today isn't going to be her day. They are ringing the doorbell like her fucking house is on fire.

"Just a minute." She pulls her robe a little tighter since she has nothing on up under it. Trinity opens the door facing two men. "How may I help you?" she asks.

"Ma'am we're sorry to bother you but we have to check your meter. He will check the one outside, I need to check the one in the house," Breeze informs her.

"Sure, come on in," Trinity let Breeze in as Craig stays outside the house. As the lookout for anyone coming. He hopes that Breeze does this shit fast because he doesn't the idea of being caught in this upscale neighborhood on bullshit.

Trinity shows Breeze to the utility closet that holds her meter. It's right off the kitchen, she made her a cup of coffee while he checks things out. An odd feeling came over her but she shook it off. As she sat at the table to sip her coffee.

Breeze is in the utility closet placing the silencer on the gun. He isn't about the rape and torture shit. That's why he told Craig to let him handle this. Breeze doesn't have time for a nigga trying to fuck the bitch before he killed her.

Alicia Howard Presents

When the bitch came to the door
she was half-dressed Craig nudges him,
Breeze ignores the nigga. This is about to
be a murder Craig would have to get
pussy on his own watch. He came out the
closet Trinity stands up to walk him to
the door.

"Is everything in order?" Trinity
asks. Breeze feels bad this woman doesn't
recognize whose business she had put
her nose in.

"Everything is fine, there's just one
more thing," Breeze says to her.

"What is that?" Trinity walks
towards him. When she saw the gun she

froze, dropping both hands with the coffee glass. Her robe fell open exposing her nude body. She doesn't know what she had done wrong, yet she hears Wesley's warning playing in her head, *"Stay out of this or you're going to get yourself killed."*

Breeze closes his eyes not wanting to see the gun destroy her beauty as he said, "This," hitting her in the chest five times. As her body flew back hitting the wall behind her. Trinity slides down the wall leaving a trail of blood. Her body is left in a sitting position. Breeze exits the house fast as he'd come.

Alicia Howard Presents

CHAPTER 26

The electric truck passed Wesley as he came down Trinity's street. He doesn't think shit of the truck. As he makes his way up the driveway. He knows that she is home because her car is there. He has been blowing her phone up. Wesley figures she wasn't answering because she is upset with him which is fine by him.

He would not let her attitude keep him from getting her to safety. Wesley hops out the car with a .45 on his hip. He has never needed a gun for anything besides, hunting since he'd been living out here. However, he made sure he keeps a few different ones in the house.

He walks up rings the doorbell. Wesley

looks around waiting to hear her call,

"Who is it." She never did.

Wesley calls her name which isn't

commonly done out here. Wesley knows

that would make her come fast. "Trinity

it's me, Wes." That is something she has

shortened his name to. He never told her

about the name WC.

He still got no response that's when

he bangs on the front door; the door

opened a little. "Fuck!" He yells because

he knows that shit is all wrong. Wesley

drops the weapon as he enters the house.

"Trinity, baby are you in here?" He walks through the massive leaving room that led to the kitchen.

"Trinity, oh God no, please no." Wesley ran to her but she was already gone. He couldn't do nothing for her. The five shots from the desert eagle had torn her entire chest cavity out. Blood leaks from her mouth from the impact of her body hitting the wall. Her eyes were wide open, looking as if they were saying, *"I am sorry."*

"Damn! Girl, why you do me like this?" Wesley cries for her. He knows that she wasn't the woman for him but she was good people. Wesley might have

treated her unfair when Hurricane came

into his life. Yet he never wanted her

harmed like this. Wesley is hugging her

and crying. When he heard sirens

coming. He knows that someone has

called the police after hearing him yelling

outside of her house.

Wesley holds her wishing he could

change the hands of time. He is still

broken from his cousin who had only

been dead six months. That's how long he

had been living out this way. The first

night he moved here is the night he

walked into the hospital. He lied to

Trinity about how he got his injuries saying he was in a motor bike accident a few miles away. Wesley had been fighting with one of the men that helped kill his cousin.

The last one wasn't going out without a fight but he was going. When Wesley told her that she believed him. Wesley knew then she was naïve. He found that cute. No matter what he will miss Ms. Dagwood.

The officers enter the house with guns drawn. Her community is so secluded the police knows people by name. "Dr. Dagwood, are you in here?"

the officer yells. He moves through the house when he heard.

"Back here," Wesley yells.

The officer ran to the area where the voice coming from. Wesley is glad he had been out there before when a fire broke out at the neighbor's house because the office remembers him. "Mr. Charleston, are you hurt?" The officer watches him hold Trinity, crying.

He knows the only thing that is broke or hurt on this man is his heart.

"She's gone, she's gone." Wesley cries like a baby. He knows the same nigga that harmed Hurricane is behind this. Out of fear of someone running around saying that Hurricane is alive cost Trinity her life. Wesley wishes that she wasn't so hard-headed. The police radios for help to come; Wesley holds her until homicide pulls him away from the body to examine the scene.

Wesley was questioned a little but the cops know they wouldn't get much information out of him. Once he was released he went home to get out of the bloody clothing. Then heads the Waldorf to holler at Hurricane. She needs to make a move before he did.

CHAPTER 27

Taz is sitting in his car outside the Rainbow Cloud getting his dick sucked by a girl name Stacey. He met her at breakfast one morning she was with Craig, Taz knew that she was checking for him. He didn't have time to entertain the idea at that moment.

Craig and Breeze had called saying the bitch is dead they are heading home. Taz is relieved now that the messy bitch was out the way. If Hurricane was alive she would have reached out to touch him by now.

Hurricane is in a black Aston Martin parked across the street from the joint. She use to park there all the time because you could see all the happenings without being notice. She has fired so many bitches for fucking outside the club.

They would think the other girls were diming them out. Hurricane father has taught her how to keep her eyes on her money. Even when people doesn't think Hurricane is watching. When Wesley suggest that she act as a ghost, she knew that he was on to something.

She was about to pull off when until she sees Breeze and Craig pulled up. Taz and the bitch jumps out the car. She could see Craig step to the girl. He is pissed; she knows that the bitch must have been one of his. Taz does this shit to him all the time, more than Hurricane could count.

That is part of the reason she would let the little nigga suck her pussy from time to time. No matter how many times Taz does this fucked up shit he would always wild out on the bitch like Taz isn't in the wrong.

Hurricane counts down to the girl's ass whooping. Ten, nine, eight, seven, six, and five... Craig punches the bitch in the face. She hit the ground as Taz and Breeze watch him, laughing as he kicks the bitch in the stomach a few times.

They all went inside the building as she lays on the ground crawling around. Once Hurricane knows the coast is clear, she swoops down on the bitch. "Get in," The girl looks at her. She looks familiar but she couldn't put her finger on where she'd seen the bitch offering her help.

Stacy jumps in the ride without thinking twice.

Hurricane hit the horn as she pulls out the parking lot. Taz, Craig, and Breeze ran outside to see honking the horn, because it the as Hurricane honked anytime she is leaving the club. Everyone knows that blow. When the black Mustang pulls off Stacy is gone, they figure it was someone she knows.

Craig looks at Taz. "That's probably that hoe's pimp," he is pissed with her for fucking with his boss.

"I'm not tripping off the car, I'm tripping off the way the horn was blown. That shit was creepy; they blew the same way Hurricane used to," Breeze says.

"I am thinking the same damn thing," Taz says adjusting his gun on his hip. He hopes that Stacy isn't trying to send no heat his way. It not his fault she got her ass whooped. He told her that Craig would be mad but she didn't care.

she was trying to come up on her rent money, Taz let her suck the dick for fifty bucks. He doesn't know how much that helps her but that is the best he could offer.

CHAPTER 28

Hurricane pushes the car. She'd seen them come out after recognizing the blow. She smiles to herself because it was time to set the plan in motion. Stacy sits in the passenger seat wondering how she could whip a bitch like this here.

Hurricane sees her starting at her. "Where are you going?" she asks her.

"6035 Broadway," Staci says proudly and shit.

Staci isn't in the projects but she wasn't too damn far from it.

Hurricane laughs. "Cool," she says before hitting the freeway.

"What's funny?" Stacey asks. She thought she was doing damn well for herself. This bitch laughing like the eleven hundred a month rent she struggling to pay isn't shit. Staci refuses to live in the damn the projects after she was eighteen.

She even left her mother behind because she has dreams outside of the projects. She is twenty now has been fucking, sucking, and setting niggas up to pay her rent. That is the only reason she ever fucked with Craig.

"Nothing. I mean it's cool if that's all you want is one foot outside of the

projects. Who I am to judge you?"
Hurricane switches gears on the Aston
Martin let that muthafucka open all the
way up on the freeway. Stacy sees that
her face is bruised up from something,

Yet she doesn't look like the bitch
that got her ass whooped. Even with the
bruised face, her swag or spirit isn't
broken like Stacy's is. She hates the way
she gets by.

"The bitch pushes a 2014 Limited
Edition Aston Martin," Stacy says out
loud.

"Excuse me?" Hurricane know what
she meant, but wants to see where her

head is at. If she really, a hoe or street bitch that hadn't been birthed yet.

"This what gives you the right to judge me," Stacy told her.

"You hungry?" Hurricane asks her.

Stacy doesn't want to come out as a hand outs. "No, I'm straight," she says, holding the fifty that Taz give her tightly in her hand. She needs all she could get for her rent. The bitch of a landlord kept posting the eviction notice on her door every morning.

If she doesn't come up with the money soon she is going to be outside on her ass.

Hurricane peeps the G in her that wants no favors she respected that. Her father taught her nothing is free. When a muthafucka offers you something, find out the motive behind the shit. "This ain't no handout, boo, this is a business meeting." Hurricanes looks at her winks.

"Well on that note, I'm down. I live for business," In Stacy's mind business meant money to her. She doesn't know what this woman is on but if it involved money, she is with it all the way.

Hurricane laughs while taking the exit before Broadway. They pulled up to the same diner that Craig took her to the day she met Taz and his girlfriend. Staci and Tammy has done a threesome with him for five thousand they split. It's a major come up because niggas aren't paying that money for shit like that considering so many were doing it for free. Therefore, when Craig made the offer, they took it.

Tammy uses to be her girlfriend back in the day. She had to cut her loose when she found out that she was fucking niggas because she liked it. Stacey only deals with niggas for money, but for love and relationships she wants a woman. Tammy told her she wanted the same but when she came up with a baby, she knew that the bitch was on something different.

They jumped out the ride as Stacy watches Hurricane. The bitch is sexy, and not cause of the money she has, but the love she has for herself is breathtaking.

Hurricane has a MK hooded scarf on her head, with Tiffany sunglass, black skinny jeans, a black biker's jacket, and a white shirt that read, *"I love bad bitches."* Of courses she has the latest J's on her feet. You could tell from the way she walks on her tiptoes she wore heels most of the time.

She walks in the diner with her held down found a booth way in the back to avoid being recognize by anyone that works there. Once seated, she looks at Stacy. "When I asked you were you hungry, I wasn't just taking about food," Hurricane school her.

"What where you speaking of then?" Stacy is all ears; something in her gut told her this is the come up she'd been waiting for.

Hurricane pulls her shades off slid the cap from her head so Stacy could see her. Stacy eyes almost popped out of her head. She is the bitch from the news that

Taz was so emotional about. Stacy has

forgotten all about Taz until the day she'd

seen him on the news. When she found

out from her home girl that the nigga

owns the Rainbow Cloud.

Staci at him, but the nigga is hella

cheap to be a boss nigga. "You're ...I

know you, from the news." Staci is too

young to know Hurricane from the streets

like most people did. Hurricane gave her

a look that silences her. Staci sat back in

her seat.

"Yes, that's me, Hurricane put her

get up back on.

"I think Taz thinks you're dead, he-e-e even has another woman." Staci stutters a little bit when she shared that. The bitch he has is gutter bucket, ratchet bitch. She doesn't see why he would be with a bitch like Rashida after having a woman like Hurricane.

"He does think this, and I am dead. Can I trust you?" Hurricane hopes that she could because she needs a woman that could get into the place of a street nigga's heart.

"Yes you can," Stacy is so eager to be a part of Hurricane's world.

"Why?" Hurricane asks her.

"Why what?" Stacy is confused.

"Why do you want to help me?" Hurricane needs to know her motive.

"Look, I am not gone lie to you. I am hoping this job involves money because that's what I need to take care of myself. I am tired of sucking and fucking these low-level niggas to get by. That shit is becoming the death of me. They're either whooping my ass or playing me out of my money.

I like bitches, but if I keep getting used and abused by these niggas, who's going to want me?" Stacy keeps it real with her Hurricane liked that.

Hurricane throws the envelope across the table to her. Stacy grabs it looking inside. She doesn't know how much money it was because she has never held that much money in her hand at one time. What she knows it's more than enough to cover her rent. "What do I have to do for this?" Stacy asks.

"Fuck with me," Hurricane told her just that calmly.

"You care to be more specific?" Stacy asks because she knew this bitch isn't giving her all this money to fuck.

"Nope, but you can start by ordering our food," she told her.

"Waiter, bring your ass over here we've been sitting here too long." Staci says. Hurricane laughs as a young girl she'd never seen there before hustles over to them to take their order.

After enjoying the meal, Hurricane drops Stacy off at her place. All she talked about over there is how she is going to pay three months on her rent. Hurricane likes her; she knows she has just gained the little sister she never had. Hurricane told Stacy to get a cell phone, and call her once she has it. Then they could get down to business.

CHAPTER 29

Wesley has been sitting in the lobby of the hotel for the past few hours once he found out that Hurricane wasn't in her room. Hurricane called him after the fallout they had earlier telling him the name the room is under if he needs her.

A black Aston Martin whips up in the parking lot. Wesley knows it's her before she even gets out. Her last car was a pink Bentley so yeah, this is her.

Hurricane hops out looking sexy as hell to him. The chill out that night was no joke as she rushes inside. When she heard "Bitches be stunting," she smiles

turning around. Wesley is part of the

reason she left the hotel today in the first

place. Hurricane needed to get her mind

off him.

"No! Street bitches do." Hurricane

looks at him noticing sadness in his eyes.

"What's the matter?" She is no longer

joking around.

"Can I come up?" Wesley asks.

"Yeah sure," He follows her to the

elevator. Wesley has seen her body but

looking at her in the light is much better.

Hurricane is a G! Looking at her you

would never think a nigga left her for dead a week ago.

Once they are in the room, he grabs Hurricane from behind kissing her neck. She moans. "Hmmm what are yoooou doing?" she asks but her panties know because they are soaking wet.

Wesley rips her jacket off, lifting up her shirt sucking on her nipples roughly. The shit felt so good Hurricane body needs this. She hasn't fucked in months. All the hoes Taz is fucking, she wasn't interested in giving him any. In her mind the rape doesn't count; that is torture.

This is the pleasure her body needs. Hurricane is so glad her flow has ended.

"Wesley, we can't do this," she says.

Wesley pushes her back on the bed yanking her pants off. "Why not?" he asks, while kissing her inner thighs. He pulls her panties to the side kissing her pussy lips just as passionately as he had the ones on her face.

Hurricane is breathing heavy. "I am; I am…." He looks at her.

"If you're about to say married I will slap the shit out of you." Wesley dives back in the pussy headfirst.

Alicia Howard Presents

"I am, I am, I am cumming,"
Hurricane says.

"Now that's the shit I want to hear."
Wesley sucks up every drop of cum that
leaks from her pussy.

"Ohhhh yassss, nasty, suck that
pussy boy." Hurricane rocks on his face
as she holds the back of his head.

Hurricane body is shaking and
twitching. Wesley got up sitting on the
bed as if he is done. "What the fuck are
you doing?" Hurricane asks him.

"I'm done I just wanted to make you
cum." Wesley lays back on the bed. Her
pussy tastes better than he imagined.

Hurricane climbs on top of him. "I want to feel it inside of me I want to be fucked." She is begging which she has never done in her whole fucking life.

"She's dead." Hurricane rolls off him onto the bed, walking the room naked.

"Who?" Hurricane doesn't understand how they went from fucking to talking about dead people.

"Trinity," he says as he covering his eyes with his hands to keep the tears from falling. That is the reason Wesley is all over her like that. He wants to take the anger out on her pussy. Wesley couldn't finish without telling her what is going on.

"The doctor? What happened?" She is loss. Who in the hell would want to kill her?

"Yes, I never told you that she saw the news, took down the number called me saying that you were married. Your husband is looking for you. I even told her the real that he tried to kill you and this was all a gimmick. She didn't believe me.

She called the people, gave them my address, and they came looking for you. I assured them I had never seen you a day in my life. After the cops left my place I felt like Trinity had gotten herself into some shit by running around saying you were alive. When I went over her house to check things out, I found her in her house dead, shot five times in the chest." Wesley is now down on his knees in front of Hurricane.

"Babe, I am sorry I never meant to bring all this drama your way. I'm sorry that I even landed in your yard. To think you in here pleasing me when I don't deserve it." Hurricane didn't like the little doctor bitch but hates this happened to her because she was trying to get Hurricane away from her man.

"It's not your fault I told her the real, she didn't listen. What more could either of us have done?" Wesley asks looking up at her.

"Trinity was trying to keep us from getting here," Hurricane says pointing to her naked body.

"Dead or not she wasn't going to be able do that. I was waiting on your body to heal. Once I thought you were well enough. I was going to take you from the guest room to my room and fuck your brains out." Wesley stands up picking her up; she wraps her legs around his waist.

"How do you know that I want you to fuck my brains out?" Hurricane kisses him passionately.

"Yo ass was just begging for this shit before a nigga started crying, getting all emotional," Wesley says smiling, showing them sexy ass gold fangs.

"You a G now?" Hurricane asks him.

"Damn right! I been a G," Wesley says still holding Hurricane around his waist.

"Make me know it." Wesley lays her on the bed flipping Hurricane on to her stomach. He enters so much dick in her she thought the muthafucka was going to come out her mouth.

They fucked so long and strong Hurricane doesn't know what time they both passed out. Her phone is ringing at 4 a.m. displaying a number she doesn't know. "Hello," She was well fucked and sleepy this call better been important.

"It's me," Stacy says into the phone.

"What's up?" Hurricane asks, forgetting that she told Stacy to call her when she got the phone. Hurricane is supposed to make a move but the dick has caused the shit to slip her mind.

"I'm at the club. Taz about to leave; he just had a fight with Rashida because she caught him and Tanya in the back sexing. He didn't know that she was coming. He kept yelling *"Didn't I tell you to stay your ass in the house?"* Then the bitch says something that I didn't like.

"You not about to be out here fucking hoes on me like you did Hurricane." I'm waiting outside to whoop the bitch ass," Stacy told her.

"No don't do that go home. You have been helpful for tonight. I'm going to hit you up later because I need to get some shit moved around," Hurricane knows the streets are dry cause Pablo Jr has been blowing her phone up. She knows that she is going to have to shit or get off the pot.

"I already I'll be waiting for your call." Hurricane hangs up thinking while Rashida is talking shit, she'd better thank Hurricane for talking Stacy out of the ass whooping she was about to get.

Wesley is sound asleep when she kisses him, and slid out the bed. Hurricane hops in the shower to freshen up quickly. She threw on a new jogging suit she has. Then she left the room heading to her house to toy with Taz's mind.

Taz was sleeping well when he feels a wet mouth on his dick. He jumps up looking around thinking he is tripping. Hurricane let herself in with a spare key that Nicole had. Hurricane is on the bed sucking the tip of his dick. As she did every morning to wake him. Before Taz could grab her head like always she slid under the bed.

Taz knows he is dreaming; hell, it would take most niggas a while to forget about that type of treatment. He jumped out of bed heading to the bathroom to piss. There is a tub full of steam hot water and lavender. Taz came flying out the bathroom; he spots his clothes laying out on the bed. With a note on them just the way Hurricane used to do it. The note read *"Love Conquers All."* Taz looks around the room then under the bed, but Hurricane was gone.

Taz hurries to put the clothing on and ran down the steps with his gun in hand. He doesn't know what the fuck is going but if a muthafucka is trying to play a joke on him. They would pay for this shit. Taz enters the kitchen heading to the back door to get to his car parked in the garage right off the kitchen.

He froze dead in his tracks when he sees the breakfast sitting in the spot he used to eat at every day. Taz knows this shit couldn't be real, but the meal has a rose and note by it. Taz is scared to touch the food but he wants to know what the note says. He slowly flipped it open it reads *"I Love U!"* Taz drops the note racing out the house so fast he fell down a few of the steps as he looks back.

Taz doesn't know what is going but he needs to get the hell out of there. Hurricane watches him speed off from the house while she is hiding in the cut; her car is parked two blocks over. Hurricane knows this neighborhood like the back of her hands. She reenters the house to do a few more things that would freak Taz out when he returns home. Hurricane made the bed, cleans the bathroom, and made his lunch placing it in the microwave. The tasks she completed has notes attached to them.

Hurricane locks the place up before making her way back through the woods to get back to her car. She calls Wesley. "Baby where are you? A nigga woke up tripping and shit," he fussed in her ear.

"I am on my way back. Would you like me to pick you up breakfast?" she asks.

"Once you get here, my breakfast is served," Wesley teased her.

"Your ass is a trip. I'm pulling up in a minute got something I need to holler at you about," Hurricane told him then hung up.

CHAPTER 30

Pablo Jr called Hurricane phone. "It's done," he informs her. Hurricane has asked him to produce a body that matches hers in height and weight but burnt beyond recognition. Place it about five miles from where the car was found. Pablo Jr even went a step further leaking so the body would be located.

"Thank you Pablo Jr., you're the best." He smiles thinking about how she has seen his best. If she'd quit playing he would give her the best nights of her life.

"Thanks gorgeous," Pablo Jr. told her.

"I know you're waiting on me to make a move to bring my sister for a visit. I'm setting up a new home for her now." Hurricane assures him she is still trying to get this money.

"I was wondering about that because mama is getting restless with the situation," Pablo Jr. warns her.

"Tell her that she will be able to come this weekend. As far as mama, I don't give a fuck how restless she's getting. She better stay put because her ass has been well taken care of for years." Hurricane is pissed this bitch ass nigga overseas is trying to the pull the rug from under her. After all the money she has put in his fucking pocket since her father died.

"That sounds like a good deal. Mama will be happy now that everything is cool. Be easy, Hurricane," Pablo Jr told her. She has the same temper he'd seen on her father when people tried to cross him. Hurricane is a pit bull in a skirt for sure.

"Thank you for everything Pablo Jr. I will never forget the love we share," Hurricane told him.

Pablo Jr wished he could tell her that love is deeper than she knows.

"Likewise babe." He ends the call and informed his father they were back in business, and Hurricane is bringing some new faces to the game.

Wesley was getting out the shower. He is heading home to look at the new house the realtor has for him. Hurricane watched his sexy ass as he got dress. She knew that she should trust no damn man right about now. Yet it is something about the man he is the real deal.

Hurricane hopes it isn't the dick talking to her. "Wesley I know you don't fuck around in the streets like you used to, but I need some men that's trustworthy that's trying to get some money."

Wesley looks at her. "Why you need my men?" he asks trying to see where her head is.

"Hell, all my men turned against me. With the fact that I am supposed to be dead. It's going to be rather hard to recruit a team. I got my bitch that will make sure that everything flows smoothly. I will be the one running shit, she will just look like she's running shit and get the credit as street queen.

"You ready to give up that title?" Wesley asks her hoping she is, because he would love to wife her. So she could see what it's like to fuck with a real nigga.

"I don't know, but I have been forced out for now. Yet I still must keep my money flowing if you feel me. I like my lifestyle," Hurricane says singing the song.

Wesley laughs at her crazy ass. "I got some boys. Let me go look at the new house and I'll get with you on that, or you could come with me to see if it's the one we, I meant I want." He plans for her to be there so he wants Hurricane to like it, too.

"I'm with that. Let me hit me my girl up to tell her we will link up at dinner

time, with a few good men to talk money,"
Hurricane told him.

Wesley shakes his head wondering
what he has his hands full with. Once
she told Stacy the deal on what was in
store for the day, she got up to get
dressed to see the house with her baby.

CHAPTER 31

Rashida is standing outside of Tanya's apartment, clowning. "Bitch come on out. You want to keep fucking my man. I got something for your bitch ass. I am nice enough to share him with your broke ass now you're steady fucking him behind my back?

Bring that ass out here; I'm about to whoop you bitch." Rashida is fed up with this shit. She had dealt through the bullshit Taz had going on with Hurricane even if it was just for the money. Rashida starting to think that is bullshit considering she is still living in the same raggedy apartment waiting for the investigation to close so she could move into the big house.

"Bitch you better get the fuck from in front of my house. You can't get mad that Taz wants a bad bitch on his arm. The only reason you are even around is because you got kids by the nigga. That's your only lifeline," Tanya hollers from the window. She may have been fucking a bitch's man and plotting a takeover, but she isn't a banger. Tanya refuse to get her face scuffed up.

"Bitch you not classy, you a man stealing, dyke stripper. You can't even cut

in a real strip club with real bad bitches."
Tanya once told Rashida the reason she
works at the Rainbow Cloud verses a
normal strip club is because it is less
competition.

Taz came whipping in the driveway
of the complex as someone called him.
However, Tanya doesn't know he was
running from that haunted ass house he
is living in. When he saw what was going
on he knows that he doesn't have time for
this shit today. He jumps out the car
Rashida spots him. "Oh bitch you called
this nigga on me, ole scary hoe," she
says.

"I didn't call him, my baby was just coming to see me," Tanya told Rashida. Taz looks at her as if she is stupid as she hung out the window blowing kisses. He thought about the shit that is taking place in the house. The damn ghost in the house he just ran out of is more useful than these two.

"Babe, I was just at the crib looking for you and one of your home girls told me you were here. Why are you clowning? You know that you're the one I want to be with. Soon as this shit is over with I'm going to make you my wife that's my word." Taz kisses her while Tanya sat in the window sticking her finger in her mouth like she was about to throw up. Her neighbors are laughing cause they all knows that she is scary but forever fucking some bitch's man or woman.

"See bitch, this is my man. You and all ya neighbors heard it." Rashida felt good Taz done this in front of everyone. He looks at Tanya hanging out the window knowing it's time to cut her off for good.

"Tanya I can't fuck with you no more. I can't let you come between my family, anymore. To make this easier on you, you're fired from the club so that way we won't have to see each other." Taz

is putting an end to this drama. He had

enough creepy shit going on around him

as it is.

"You heard that, bitch? You're fired

straight like that." Rashida is doubling

over laughing. She feels sorry for the hoe

after all she has done for Tanya, but she

should not have tried to play her like

that.

"Taz I need my fucking job, I got to

pay my rent." Tanya is hanging out the

window crying. Taz walks Rashida to her

car so she could get the hell out here as

his phone rang. He sees the Missing

Person Alert number which caused him to yell at her. "Bitch get in the fucking car take your ass home." She jumps in the car speeding off with the quickness.

Taz hates treating her like that but it is the only time she listens for real. He looks up to the window at Tanya while shaking his head get back into his car to dial the last call back.

The worker picks up. "Mr. Blackmon, how are you today?" she asks him.

"I could be doing better, what made you call?" Taz wonders is someone else claiming to see Hurricane. Taz thinks the woman he had killed was telling the truth. The person house she sent them to had lied. Taz is going to have Craig and Breeze go pick up the owner of that house and bring them to him for questioning.

"I'm sorry, but I think we have found your wife. She's dead and severely burnt. We need you to come down to the hospital to identify the body," she informs him. She knows this poor man is ready for all of this to be over with so he could move on with his life.

"I will be there soon as possible," Taz told her.

He got on the phone calling Breeze; that nigga picks up sounding as if he losing his mind. "Hello," he said too quickly, talking paranoid.

"Man, what's wrong with you?" Taz asks him.

"Nothing man, just tripping off some shit that's been going on today." Breeze rubs his head, holding the rose and note he found on his car this morning.

"Man I feel you. I've had some strange shit happen at my house, too," Taz told him.

"Really? Like what?" Breeze asks.

Alicia Howard Presents

Taz ran down all the shit that took place. Breeze almost drop the phone; he doesn't know what the fuck is going on. "Man you still there, everything okay?" Taz asks him.

"Man I'm here, but I got a note and rose that was on my car in Hurricane's handwriting saying "Enjoy Your Day Friend." She used to leave him that kind of note daily with a flower.

"Are you fucking serious? I just got a call to come claim the body. Once I wrap this shit up, I'm going to find the sick fuck behind these sick ass jokes, man." Taz doesn't understand what is going on.

Taz ends the call with Breeze once he assured him they would go to the house where that doctor chick said she saw Hurricane bring the owner back to Taz as he ordered.

Taz pulled up to the hospital hoping it's really Hurricane they have found.

CHAPTER 32

Taz looks over at the body wondering if it's her, and how did she get burnt up? He would not go that far. Taz tries to find the tattoo on her hip this body is damn near charred. He doesn't care if it was her or not, Taz is ready to put this shit behind him.

He has enough shit going on in his life with Rashida, Tanya, the ghost in his house not mention the fact he still has no plug to supply the streets.

Taz don't understand street business for real; it's not always about the money, it's about the loyalty. He just knew with Hurricane out the way Pablo Jr. would get in bed with him on getting money, yet it's not that simple.

Hurricane's father is the reason she is entitled to this plug. Taz has no one to vouch for him in the streets. Hurricane is the first person that ever tried to helping him get money. This is the way he repaid her.

Taz looks at the body wanting to feel sorry but he doesn't. He watched her all his life even though Hurricane never even noticed him; she was too busy riding in her Range Rover at fifteen to remember that he is the son of the last woman her father dated.

Taz mother was head over hills in love with Heavy, yet he didn't see her as nothing more than an easy fuck and a place to train his new runners. Taz used to ask him to let him get down with the team, but Heavy always told him no.

He said he had no street sense. Taz was the young boy that played a lot and Heavy couldn't have that on his watch. A stickup boy would have killed him so fast it would have been funny.

Taz's mother used to cry and beg Heavy to take her out the hood. He told her he had only done that for one woman in his lifetime, and that no one could replace her. Heavy gave her more than enough money for her to move whenever she liked. Yet she would waste the money with her girlfriends. She didn't even buy clothing for Taz like she should have.

That is the main reason Hurricane's father wasn't willing to put her on a wife level. She was a bottom feeder no amount of money can change that.

Taz blamed Heavy for his mother's shortcomings because he felt like she loved Heavy more than she did him. That was true but Heavy wasn't the blame - his mother was.

Taz stares at the body more; he hates her; he has always hated her. The sight of Hurricane makes his skin crawl; to him she is nothing but a spoiled hood rich bitch. Her father gave her the fucking world. Yet Taz doesn't even know his father.

That nigga shook his mother the moment he found out she was pregnant. Taz mother did what she had to do for them more for so her. She hustled for Heavy was down with that nigga for over sixteen years, but it didn't mean shit to him. She even accepted the fact the she wasn't his woman alone. It didn't change the way he felt about her. Taz understood that now cause no matter what Hurricane did he still sees her in the same light. Even after the death of her father, she still has it all.

Taz would never forget the day his mom was killed. She had started using the heroin she had been selling all these years. She used it to ease the hurt Heavy caused her, not realizing that she was hurting herself more. She got real high one night after she had stabbed Heavy five times, a few days prior in a bar.

She was high when she'd done that shit to him. She got away, but evidently not far enough. She was at the local corner store sitting on a stoop talking shit about what she had done. *"Yeah I killed the cheap bitch, had all that got damn money and wouldn't give me shit,"* she *said in and out of nods.*

She hadn't noticed Hurricane following her, nor did she see her coming. Taz's mom realized she had fucked up once the bullet pierced her brain; her eyes popped open as her body hit the ground. Hurricane looks at the people standing around.

As she stared at them, they all took off running. The bitch never saw the inside of a jail for this cause no one would name her, yet they all know that she did it.

Taz vowed to make her pay for taking the only somebody he had in this world. He doesn't realize tears has fallen from his face until the person that allows you to view the body hands him a tissue. "I'm sorry for your loss." She walks back to her desk marking the body as Heather Douglas Hurricane.

"I'm sorry for my loss, too." Taz walks out the room ready to take over the world. He knows the Escobar's aren't fucking with him, but with a death certificate, every dime Hurricane have would be turned over to him. As far as he is concerned, he doesn't need the plug; soon enough he could fly over there to get his own shit.

Taz left the building with a smile so big that strangers on the street wonders what he is so happy about. He jumps in his ride to get his family and bring them home. He doesn't want to sleep in that spooky house ass one more night alone.

Taz thought about Rashida; she is his ride or die boo. After all the shit he

Alicia Howard Presents

has put her through it's well over due for

him to make all of her dreams come true.

CHAPTER 33

Craig and Breeze heads out to do what Taz asks them to do. The car ride was silent for a while when Craig asks, "When you talk to Taz, did he say anything about getting one of them little funny notes that Hurricane used to leave us?" When Craig found the note laying on his bed, he almost jumped out of his body.

Breeze damn near flipped the damn car over when he asks that. Swerving all over the highway, he took a minute to gain control of the car again. "Man what the fuck is wrong with you?" Craig hates wearing seatbelts, but not knowing what the hell Breeze is on, he grabs it quick fast and locking himself in.

"Man my bad, it just caught me off guard because he did say some strange shit was happening at the house. I also got a note from her today too." Breeze doesn't like this shit one bit. He doesn't know if they are battling a damn ghost or a human.

"I got one, too. The muthafucka was just laying on my bed like someone had been in my spot. Man, this shit is crazy. I think them niggas that ran off playing a sick ass joke on us. If I catch one of them muthafuckas in my house, I swear I'm doming their ass." Craig doesn't like his mind to be fucked with. Even though he is trying to place the blame somewhere else, it was somewhat hard to.

His note read, "Come taste me." Hurricane would leave him little notes and shit like that when she was alive. He would tear them up so Taz wouldn't know that he was sucking his wife's pussy from time to time.

"I feel you on that shit; I didn't think about the fact it could be them niggas. I hope they ain't on no hoe shit like that,"

Breeze said like the shit they had done to Hurricane was all-good.

They pulled up to Wesley's house which looked dark as hell as if it could be empty, they both got out the car with weapons drawn just in case this was some shady shit that Taz was on to knock them. They were down with him but no one is to be trusted. "Man this place looks as if no one lives here," Craig says.

"I was thinking the same damn thing my nigga." Breeze is peeking through the window of the place as Craig joined him to make sure that he saw no movement going on.

"Damn this place is dope. This the type of shit I plan to buy when we start getting this money." Craig is excited about the come up that has yet to come. Breeze isn't stressing that shit; he has a little nest egg put away. If Taz didn't come up on a plug soon he relocating on their asses. He would not tell Craig that cause the nigga might dime him out before he could make his move.

"I feel you son, we just got to lock a plug down nigga. Its dry as hell out here since Hurricane was killed. Niggas are pissed with Taz for fucking with the money so he better find a way to fix this shit soon." Breeze schools him on the word on the street.

"I been hearing that niggas are tight. A couple muthafuckas even been out robbing cats," Craig informs him. He doesn't tell he that he is one of the niggas pulling capers around this bitch. With all that big time stunting he be doing, that nigga doesn't have shit stacked away.

He needs to come up quick. Craig even been looking for low budget work in the streets but no one had any. They were all fucking with Hurricane.

"Niggas is starving out here family," Breeze told him as he spots a "Sold" sign. "Bruh look at this shit." Craig came to check things out.

"Well I'll be damned, they done sold the fucking house." He has his hands on his waist wondering what is going on. This shit just isn't adding up. Why would the doctor bitch give them a lead to an empty house? The bitch couldn't have needed the five G's that bad.

"Well let's go school your boy on the matter at hand here." Breeze walks back to the car.

"Nigga let's grab a bite to eat, too, cause all this inspector gadget shit got a nigga hungrier than a muthafucka." Craig jumps in the whip hoping soon they would be fucking bad bitches and getting money.

CHAPTER 34

Hurricane and Stacy sits at the round table in the meeting hall of the Waldorf. Hurricane booked this room for the business meeting she needs to take place so she could put money back into the streets. She had called Stacy so she could be there before Wesley bought in his men.

Stacy wasted no time getting there; she walks in with a pinstriped pencil skirt, white blouse, reading glasses, flawless flowing hair, and black Red Bottom six-inch heels. She told her to come dress liked an executive, but the bitch is beat. Hurricane is surprised and proud of the young girl; she knows their ride would be a long one.

"Well damn Miss Stacy, look at you," she teased her. Hurricane didn't realize the kid has so much ass on her. The girl has body for days to be as tall as she is.

Stacy is five foot ten, caramel, no stomach, forty-four D breast with enough hips and ass to feed a small country. Hurricane doesn't know how she missed that ass. This child will make you ask *"K Michelle, who?"*

"Do you really like it? I hope I didn't overdo it?" Staci has never dressed like an executive, but when she saw this naughty librarian on a movie she watched her saying that is the look she would try for the meeting.

"Baby you killed this shit. If I was into bitches, you would be mine, no questions asked." Hurricane meant every word she said to her.

"Thank so much boss lady," Stacy blushed.

"No, *you're* the boss lady now, I'm just the plug. I have had my run; now that the world thinks I'm dead, I can lay low for a while but I still want this money, you feel me?" Stacy nods her head yes. She wants to make sure she understood everything Hurricane is telling her. Stacy never planned to go from a low-level bitch to the boss in a few days.

This is overwhelming, but she would not let Hurricane down. Any girl from the hood would have loved to take this job but she chose her, so she plans to make her proud.

"I don't know if I can replace…" Hurricane cut her off. The last thing she needs is for Stacy to doubt herself.

"You don't have to replace me I am dead. You will be better than me. I fucked up by letting a broken heart lead me into the hands of a fuck nigga. That won't happen to you because one, you like bitches, and you will keep your bitches in order. If she ain't classy enough to respect your title, you don't want the bitch." Hurricane was boosting her ego as she fed her brain.

"I am the new street bitch queen." Stacy looks at Hurricane with a half smirk on her face. Stacy never wanted to be the street queen but wanted to get money; finding a job isn't always easy.

The things her heart desired, a normal job couldn't provide.

"That's what the fuck I'm talking about. When these niggas come up in here you gotta make them know you run things. If you don't they will think they can run over you," Hurricane told her.

"I got it," Stacy says smiling from ear to ear.

"I'm just the plug sell them on that shit baby. After the meeting I got something for you." Hurricane kisses her cheek smacking her on the ass. When she walks past her to get the men. Stacy blushed.

She knows that Hurricane doesn't like women but she might change her mind. Even if she never makes her hers,

she will get to taste that pussy one day.

CHAPTER 35

Hurricane is wearing a black jump suit mostly because she'd still be sexy while she hid the ace bandage around her ribs. She had to put it on; today the pain was on a thousand due to all the dipping and sliding she did when she was at her house fucking with Taz's head.

Hurricane cream, thigh high boots clicks the pavement causing heads to turn as Hurricane walks as if she were ripping the runway on the Waldorf Hotel. Wesley is sitting at the bar when Zeke nudges him. "Nigga look." He thought

Hurricane was the baddest bitch he'd ever seen in his life.

Wesley looks to see what his cousin is on. "Yeah, she cute," he says as she walked in his direction.

"Cute? Nigga, you out your fucking mind! That bitch is bad look at her! You *know* she got her own muthafuckin money. If she stops by us I'm jumping down on her. She a little out of my league but I'm going for mines fuck that. I got to." Zeke is a young wild ass nigga that keeps a bad bitch, but never one on Hurricane's level.

"I feel you nigga if you don't get at the sexy muthafucka, I am," Yayo says, jumping in the conversation. He was checking her out, knowing damn well Hurricane wouldn't look at this silly ass twice; not because he is unattractive, because he plays too much.

"Man sit y'all thirsty asses down. That bitch married to some millionaire, she doesn't want y'all asses," Blaze fussed. He doesn't have time to be looking at that hoe he is waiting for the meeting to get this paper.

"Shut the fuck up, Blaze! Your ass just mad because you can't have the

bitch with yo 'married with children' ass."
Smooth clowns him as they all burst out
laughing.

Smooth wasn't checking for her
because he thinks he is the shit. In his
mind he is a rich woman's fantasy, and
poor woman's dream. These are Wesley's
rounds. He has history and love for all
these niggas.

Wesley is leaning back on the bar
when Hurricane slid between him and
Zeke. She kisses him as all the men eyes
bulged out. They are used to Wesley's
chicks being proper, but this some next
level bad bitch shit.

"Baby, are your men here for the meeting?" Hurricane asks. She has never meet them.

Wesley grabs her by the waist pulling her close to him nibbling at her neck. "Yeah sexy, they're ready." He is looking dope in the all black True Religion button down shirt, pants, black Gucci sneakers, and black fedora with a cream feather in it. Yeah, his dope boy swag was on a thousand tonight.

"You a dirty muthafucka cuz, letting us check for this bitch knowing that she is yours." Zeke says licking his lips. His cuz has come a long way from the hoes in the hood.

"It's Ms. Bitch to you sir, and I am not his, he mines." Hurricane walks toward the meeting hall.

"Excuuuuse me, Ms. Bitch," Zeke teases as she cut her eyes at him. He smiles sharing the most amazing dimples she'd seen.

"Nigga don't be showing off them pretty ass dimples she mines." Wesley pulls him in for a hug. It feels good to be around the crew; he hasn't seen them since Twan died. Zeke is Twan's baby brother. They looked so much, he feels like he is hugging a ghost.

CHAPTER 36

"Oh shit Taz fuck this pussy, fuck it hard," Tanya moans.

"Grrrghh. Throw that pussy back bitch, throw it back on this dick," Taz growls. He knows that he said that he wasn't fucking her anymore, but her pussy is soooo good. She came by the club to clean out her locker and stopped by the office on the way out to apologize for how she behaved with Rashida.

The apology led to dick sucking, and fucking on his desk. Tanya knew what she was doing. She needs to keep this nigga in the pocket she will do whatever it takes. "Oh daddy I want to feel it in my ass, please put in my ass, baby." Tanya is an ole freaky nasty ass bitch. That's why Taz couldn't cut her off, as he should.

He slides the head of his dick up in her ass "Augggghh." Taz eyes rolled into the back of his head because that ass is so fat, and juicy just like her pussy, but ten times tighter. Taz could remember the few times Hurricane let him get that ass.

It wasn't often but memorable. That is the only time he liked the bitch. Taz forgot that he wasn't fucking Hurricane pounding Tanya's asshole like crazy. "You like getting that ass fucked huh, ole

freaky bitch huh! Talk to me Hurricane."
He busted all in Tanya ass.

She is pissed that he thought about the bitch he killed while fucking her. It showed her just how much she meant to him. He even loved the dead bitch more than he did her, though he tried to make his mind believe he hates Hurricane.

"Aww shit, Hurricane," Taz says for the second time.

"I am not Hurricane." Tanya jumps off his desk pulling her pants up.

Taz opens his eyes to find Tanya. He is tripping bad. "I'm sorry, boo. You know sometimes names come out when you're so used to being with that person." Taz tried to clean the shit up.

"It's cool. I'm not your bitch I just enjoy the dick. I hope the little freak session helps me get my job back." Tanya mouth played it cool though her heart sang a different tune. She loves the shit out of Taz, but it's not about what he has, it's how he is.

She doesn't know the monster that killed Hurricane. She knows the man that would come to her house late night with strawberries, wine, and give her a full body message for working so hard in the club. Then fucking her until she cried herself to sleep.

"I can't let you work here, Rashida wouldn't be happy about that. If you promise to leave the light on for me, I will make sure you have everything you need," Taz promises her cause he loved her too. But Rashida has his loyalty and children there is no walking away from that. Taz hands her ten stacks.

"I will always keep the light on for you, daddy." Tanya leans over the desk kissing him passionately. He closes his eyes as he felt the love spill from her.

Craig and Breeze came in on the kiss. "Oh shit we'll come back," Breeze says.

"No the hell we won't, that bitch better bounce." Craig doesn't like her for the same reason he helped kill Hurricane. She is stingy with the pussy. At least Hurricane fed the nigga from time to time. This bitch wouldn't even let him smell it. He is tired of the hoes always wanting a boss nigga.

Tanya rolled her eyes at Craig and kissed Breeze on the cheek before replying "I am leaving." She grabs her bags heading home. If Taz took care of her as he promised he would, to hell with this club. Tanya would open up her own beauty shop. She has a plan to keep him. Taz loves kids so much she should give him one. She made a mental note to set up an appointment to have her IUD removed.

After Taz made her have the last abortion, she had the IUD put in place to avoid killing another child.

"Where the hell she going looking like a bag lady?" Breeze asks. He has never see her with that many clothing on to have that many bags.

"She retiring," Taz lied. There is no need to put his or her personal business on blast. Something is telling him he would like their relationship much better this way. He has always had more than one bitch. Rashida wanting him to change now isn't clear to him.

She had better be happy with the new throne she is sitting up on. No one can have everything. Most women that got a nigga with money won't have a faithful man, too.

"Yeah fucking right, that bitch lives for this place; her ass got fired. Rashida isn't having that shit. Only a blind man couldn't see that was coming," Craig rambled on. Craig has been telling Rashida what was going on with Taz and Tanya behind her back. It had nothing to do with him wanting to fuck her; she isn't classy enough for him. He just wanted the bitch Tanya to pay for playing him.

"Man, shut the fuck up! Did y'all find out what was up with that place the doctor bitch had me send the people to?" Taz is trying to get clarity on that strange shit happening around him.

"Man, that muthafucka sold," Craig informs him.

"Aye, Craig got one of the little funny notes, too, family." Breeze's big mouthed ass had to bring the shit up. He didn't want to talk about that, plus his phone is jumping like crazy from the nigga Blaze he was trying to get work from. Craig pockets couldn't wait on Taz.

"Word up? What did it say, family?" Taz know she left every one little funny notes; it was just her thing. Most of the niggas found it cute, wishing they a bitch did shit like that. Taz had gotten used to it over the years.

"You know that ole 'drive with love' ass shit." They all burst out laughing.

Craig had to come up with something. He couldn't tell the nigga what it said. Taz believed him because even though Hurricane is a street bitch she has a Mary Poppins vibe to her.

"Damn I'm going to miss her," Breeze slips and says in the moment of reminiscing. Silence fell upon the room cause in their own right, they all would.

"Well, I got to get up out of here." Craig is glad Breeze has his car parked in the club lot. Money is calling he has to answer, cause his bills are past due, and he hasn't fucked in a few weeks.

"Yeah, I identified the body. Hurricane is officially dead. Now I'm heading home to my family," Taz says. He had moved Rashida and the children in. Rashida wasted no time packing up Hurricane's shit. She plans to throw out the things she couldn't squeeze into.

"I am going to a real strip club where the bitches like dick or a little bit of both." Breeze couldn't believe that Taz has moved the family in already, but that isn't his problem. He needs to be fucked, with all the stupid shit going on around him.

Alicia Howard Presents

They all had been through some shit in the past two weeks. I hope this shit is all behind them now that Hurricane is official pronounced dead.

CHAPTER 37

The meeting was great. Stacy wrapped it up by telling the men the first shipment is due to come in tonight. They had to meet her at the warehouse that Hurricane got for her. Hurricane had Nicole cancel the lease on the one Taz knows about.

While Hurricane sits watching Stacy do her thing, she knew that she has picked well.

Stacy slips on her jacket, heading to meet the carrier to get the shipment so she could own the streets. Before she could leave, Hurricane walks over to her. "Hey love, you did an amazing job."

"Thank you sis! You're not gone leave me out here alone, are you?" Stacy wants this job but she didn't know shit about killing. She plans on taking shooting lessons knowing she would have to have her own back, because sometimes the muthafucka that's supposed to protect you is the same muthafucka that kills you.

Hurricane told her she needs to be better than her; that is a helluva task, but she is up for it.

"Baby I am one call away from you, and you're never alone out there. I got too comfortable in my life trusting the wrong people. Two years after my husband talked me into getting rid of my body guard, the bitch ass nigga tried to kill me." Hurricane had to laugh at the shit.

She thought he loved her so much he would make sure she was safe, at least the what Taz told her. *"Why are you paying them when you got me?"* Taz would asked her. She let him talk her into giving them up.

Hurricane should have listened to her father when he told her *"People whose family you feed will keep you safer than a muthafucka that claims to love you."*

"Cool! Again, thank you for everything," Stacy says to her as Hurricane hugs her.

"Let me walk you out." Hurricane know she needed a place in the city close to Stacy. They got outside the hotel as Wesley is coming from seeing the crew off. He is glad his boys were about to be getting that big boy money. Wesley isn't going to be getting a bad cut either.

The valet pulls up with the Aston Martin handing Stacy the keys. "I'm sorry, this not my car." she doesn't own a no car yet.

"Yeah, that right there is you," Hurricane told her. Stacy looks at her as if she is crazy. She doesn't understand why this woman is doing all this for her. Stacy has never had anyone treat her this well, not even her own mother. She was too busy getting drunk to treat anyone or anything well outside of that bottle.

"I don't know what to say," Stacy says. She is lost for words.

"If I were you, I would park it in my garage," Wesley told her, He knows what

Hurricane has done he thought it was the dopiest shit ever.

"I don't have a garage," Stacey says to him as she looks at the car. She couldn't believe it. Her first fucking car is a 2014 Aston Martin. Now that's a fucking upgrade for your ass. She doesn't know how she would repay this woman, but she plans to die trying

"Yes you do." Hurricane hands her the key to Wesley's old house. Hurricane bought it when Wesley bought the new one, not liking the place Stacy lives in. It isn't fitting for the new street queen.

The key has the address on the disposable key ring. She has never felt so special or loved as she feels at this moment. Hurricane know that she needed this life when she seen her let a nothing ass nigga like Craig treat her like shit.

Hurricane know this Stacy doesn't know her worth, for real. Hurricane needed someone to be the face of her business so she handpicked someone they never would expect.

Stacy is about to cry. "Thank you." Stacy admires the person Hurricane is and doesn't know how she expected her to be better than she is.

"Street bitches don't cry," Hurricane reminds her.

Stacy kisses her on the lips. "No we don't." She hops in the whip to get the shipment, but she really couldn't wait until she could see her new home.

Wesley looks at Hurricane. "So this why you bought this heifer all this shit? She just going to kiss my bitch in front of me," He jokes.

"I bet it made you horny," Hurricane says while licking his lips.

"Damn sure did." Wesley dick is so hard had it been glass, the muthafucka would have broken.

"Shall we fuck?" Hurricane got classy on him remembering they were at the Waldorf Astoria Hotel.

"We shall." He says Hurricane takes off running into the hotel as he chased behind her. Wesley doesn't know when or how he has fallen in love, but he did.

CHAPTER 38

Nicole told Hurricane she would meet with Taz in the morning for reading the will. He wastes no time contacting they lawyer she told him to call if something ever happened to her. He told the facility to have the body cremated and send him the bill.

When the summons came in for Nicole saying she had to be at reading the will, she wonders what hell is going on. She knows it's early but she has to call her girl. Hurricane hit her Bluetooth.

"Hello," she whispers thinking it was Wesley. She had fucked him to sleep again. Then left him in the bed to go Taz's house.

"Bitch why do I have to go to the reading of the will?" Nicole asks. She doesn't want Taz's crazy ass knowing what the fuck she looks like. If a man will kill his wife, he might want to kill her banker, too.

"Because," she whispered again.

"Because what? Why are you fucking whispering?" Nicole knows that Wesley can't be that light of a sleeper, even if he were, Hurricane wouldn't care that damn much.

"Because the court order told you to." She didn't want to tell her what this is all about. She going to have to wait and see. She swore Nicole is black sometimes considering how nosey she is.

"I'm whispering because I am 'Casper the Street Bitch' ghost. I'm in my old house cleaning up. He done moved this nasty bitch and kids in my shit." Hurricane got loud for a minute.

"Girl, you are fucking kidding me?" Nicole couldn't believe that trifling ass nigga would pull shit like this. That nigga is a cold muthafucka.

"I didn't even know the bitch had kids you dig, but I am going to send that hoe to the mental hospital, you watch. I'm going to make both of their asses suffer." Hurricane's voice drips with ice.

"I feel you bitch. Let me get my dumb ass ready for this hearing somebody done drug me into," Nicole yells into the damn phone. She would have to call her job tell them she would be late because she has a hearing reading her grandmother's will.

They would be glad cause she has left the office early too many times to count, for her ill grandmother only to be

going to a sale at Nordstrom's.

"Bitch, I love you too." She hung up

so she could finish the shit before Taz

woke up.

Alicia Howard Presents

The sun shines through the window of Taz's bedroom alerting him it's time to get up. Rashida is up under him asleep after the great fuck session they had last night. Part of Taz felt like he is greedy by fucking two women in one night, knowing he was offering one the rest of his life. Taz shakes his head. No, he isn't greedy he is the man.

He wished Rashida would have pulled the blinds at night like Hurricane used to do; he hates being awakened by the morning sun. Rashida would have to get on her womanly duties, cause this shit isn't normal or right in Taz's world.

Alicia Howard Presents

He went downstairs to have some cereal Rashida brought. Taz doesn't want to be hungry on this big day of his. Today is the day he would finally get to find out how much this bitch is really holding. He spots the cereal in the trash with a note. *"Kings don't eat childish things."*

"Taz bumps into the counter knocking over orange juice he never realized was on the table next to a plate with grits, bacon, eggs, and wheat toast. He grabs a towel to clean up the juice then ran over to the breakfast to see what that note says. Hurricane watches him fumble around the kitchen. The closer he got to her, the closer she moved to the foyer.

Taz read the note. *"Eat up big plans today."* He walks around the kitchen yelling, "Stop playing with me bitch. If you're alive, show yourself." He is freaking out. Rashida heard him yelling she came running down the steps in Hurricane's favorite robe.

Hurricane looked at her thinking *The nerves of this bitch to rock a dead woman's shit.*

"Baby, what's the matter?" Rashida asks a terrified looking Taz.

"This! All of this." He waves his hand around. Rashida noticed the spilled juice and cooked food.

"Did you clean up?" she asked, because she know damn well she hadn't. She planned to speak with him today about getting a maid and a nanny. Rashida would not be stuck up in the house all day when there is much needed shopping she needs to be doing.

"No, this is her, this is all her," Taz yells.

"Who?" Rashida doesn't understand what is going on.

Alicia Howard Presents

"Hurricane! I know it's her doing all this shit. She ain't dead! We gotta move babe." Taz is scared shitless.

"Nah, we ain't moving. That bitch is dead you got the death certificate. I haven't even had a chance to give any parties here yet." Rashida isn't running away from a ghost. She will call her aunt Bessie for some blessed oil first.

The door slammed causing Taz and Rashida to jump. Taz grabs the heat he kept in the kitchen drawer before going to check out what it was. The glass in the door is shattered. As if someone has just walked out of it. A note is mingled in the glass he picked up, but it was addressed to Rashida. "A tidy home makes a husband happy." She looks at shit around the house not knowing what the fuck is going on here.

Hurricane made it back to her car mad as hell. The nerve of the two simple muthafuckas laying up in her shit. Little did they know, that bitch is going on the market to be sold.

Hurricane know that Breeze is laid up at Motel Six with a little stripper bitch he got from Pumps. She swung back by there to put a note in his car using a master key she had retrieved. Hurricane had been to his house last night before she came to bother Taz. Breeze has shit in motion to leave town he narrowed down where he is going. It didn't matter to her where the fuck he <u>went</u>; she is going to drive him insane until she is ready to touch him.

Hurricane had enough fun for one morning. So she heads back to the hotel to talk to Wesley about having his realtor finding her a place in the city. The Waldorf is a beautiful place, but she needs a place to call home. It has to be plush because she would spend enough time in it.

Alicia Howard Presents

Taz came to the meeting forty-five minutes late looking a mess. He has been drinking with worn, wrinkled clothing. Hurricane had set his clothing out but he refused to put them on. His head is spinning behind this bullshit. Rashida could keep playing if she wants to, she is going to be living in that bitch by her damn self if this shit keeps happening.

"Mr. Blackmon, glad that you could make it. We were about to read the will without you," Timothy Huge told him. Huge is Hurricane's attorney and potna. This dope white boy is sweet on sisters. He used to always tell Hurricane *"A white bitch can't do shit for me but introduce me to her black friend."* That is how he got the black wife he was now through her white friend.

"Well I'm here now muthafucka, so read this shit," Taz scolded before looking at Nicole wondering who this white bitch thought she is. She is sexy ass for sure. If Taz had her down at the club, that bitch would be packed like a muthafucka.

Shit, for this bitch he might even let niggas in. Nicole has jet black hair, green eyes, full lips, and a body like Chloe Kardashian.

Alicia Howard Presents

"I will be more than glad to, sir."

Timothy looks at this bitch ass nigga with a disgust he couldn't hide. He doesn't understand nothing ass nigga that wants to have shit they didn't earn. The sight of this nigga makes Huge sick to his stomach.

He thought to himself, *"Let me get this lame ass nigga out my office, before I have one of my cop homies knock his ass."* Timothy read the will:

"LAST WILL AND TESTAMENT:

A married person's will, leaving the residue of the estate to the surviving spouse and providing for guardianship of minor children. Seeing as how I never had any here is how I leave my will.

Will of <u>Heather Douglas Blackmon</u>

I, <u>Heather Blackmon</u> also known as Hurricane and/or formerly known as Heather Douglas of Bronx County, NY declare this my last will and testament.

I.   I revoke all previous wills and codicils.

II. I am married and my name is <u>Heather Blackmon</u>. All references in this will to my husband are to <u>Tazavaes Blackmon</u>.

III.   If no children: I have no children, living or dead.

IV.   I direct that my funeral be conducted <u>Our Lady of Mt. Carmel Church</u> by Pope John Paul at 627 E 187th St, Bronx, NY 10458.

V.   I direct that my body be buried in my_family_plot in the <u>Saint Raymonds Cemetery</u> at <u>2600 Lafayette Ave Bronx, NY.</u>

VI.   I direct that the total cost of my funeral, burial, and gravestone is not to exceed fifty thousand Dollars ($<u>50,000</u>).

VII. It is my intention by this will to dispose of my individually owned property and my devisable interest in any other property. *I do not intend to exercise any power of appointment which I may have.*

VIII. I give to my husband, <u>Tavares Blackmon</u>, no rights of interest I may have in my home, at Chestnut Hill Dr. Bronx, NY or any other home which we may occupy as our principal residence at my death, subject to any trust, deed or other encumbrance and all unpaid

real property taxes and special

assessments which are a lien

at the date of my death.

IX.   I give to my friend, Nicole

Walsh, all interest I may have

in all household furniture,

furnishings, fixtures, jewelry,

china, silverware, books,

pictures, clothing, and all other

items of domestic, household

or personal use or adornment,

and all automobiles which at

the time of my death shall be

in, about, or used in connection with my home.

X.   All the residue of my estate must leave within sixty days. Property over which I may have a power of appointment I give to my friend Nicole Walsh, right to the said property as see she fit.

XI.   My executor may, at his sole discretion, retain any securities, real property, or other investments, and continue to hold, manage, and operate any property, business, or enterprise I may

own in whole or in part during

my death, with or without

order of court, the profits or

losses therefore to inure to and

be chargeable against my

estate and not my executor.

XII. I direct my executor to pay all

my just debts, the expenses of

my last illness and funeral and

burial expenses when it is

legally possible to do so.

XIII. All estate, inheritance,

succession, or other death

taxes, duties, charges or

assessments, imposed on or in relation to any property by my death, whether passing under this will or otherwise, shall be paid by my executor out of the residue of my estate, without proration of any charge therefore against any person who receives such property under the terms or otherwise.

XIV. I appoint Timothy Hughes, attorney and counselor at law, of 678 Lenox, New York County, NY, as the attorney for my executor.

XV.   I sign my name to this will on 10/27/13, at 678 Lenox New York County, NY, in the presence of Timothy Huge, Samantha Huge, and Tangier White, attesting witnesses, who subscribe their names hereto at my request and in my presence.

Once Timothy got done reading the will, you could see smoke coming out of Taz's ears He is mad as hell. He thought killing this bitch would make his life better, but his life is becoming a living hell Taz lost everything behind this shit.

Alicia Howard Presents

Hurricane would not beat him in death, even if it kills him he plans to come out on top.

CHAPTER 39

Blaze linked up with Craig because he had been bugging him about getting this money. He was telling Blaze how Taz fell off and he isn't eating with him. He explains how he doesn't want to live under handed, but he has to feed his family. Blaze know what all about being that he is thirty the father of two girls.

Blaze's family meant the world to him, that is why he is out here in these streets to pay for his wife to go to law school. She wasn't letting them babies stop her, and he admired her for that.

There aren't many strong women in the world today; they all want to be thots and hoes, posting on Instagram and shit. His shorty isn't in to any of that; she had made class or so he believes.

Craig pulls up on the nigga finally after a whole fucking day has passed.

"What's up baby?" Craig said jumping into Blaze's whip.

"You a day late, I hope you not a dollar short." Blaze is a family man and killer. He is not to be fucked over. He is most definitely the nigga that is going to get you before you got him.

Being level headed always keeps him one-step above the next muthafucka. Just like now if Craig looks like he wants to flex. There's muthafucka waiting to take his head off.

"Aww family, never that, I just don't ride dirty like that. You gotta show me a sample of what you working with. Then we can make arrangements for the near future.

Blaze reached in his pocket handing a pinch of what he has to offer. He knows that Craig is his own tester for the product, that's why he stays broke. Most of his money was is going up his nose and on the hoes. Blaze feels bad for the man, but he isn't going to stop him from spending his money with him. "May I?" Craig asks if he could take little taste in the man car. Everyone doesn't allow that shit.

"Do your thing, pimpin'." Blaze is ready for the nigga to get the fuck out of his car. He doesn't trust niggas like that, Zeke is on that rooftop with the scope, he is cool.

"Ouch," Craig hollers; that shit has grabbed him. He doesn't know that is going to fuck up his whole life.

"You like?" Blaze asked, shaking his head because the nigga is already leaning.

"Yeah, yeah, that shit straight. What's the price?" Craig asked.

"17.5, no shorts." Blaze is on it.

"Damn that's a plug! I'll call you in an hour so to link up and get that," Craig told him nodding some more.

"Get the fuck out my car, call me when your money's right." Blaze told him.

"Alright nigga. I'll get with you in a minute baby." Craig hops out as Blaze drove off before he could even close the door. Hurricane has ordered him to fuck with Craig to see what is shaking on their end.

Craig watches Blaze speeding away he knows the shit the nigga has is pure, but he wants to know who is holding. He doesn't ask because he know damn well Blaze isn't going to tell him that.

Therefore, he opted to sit back and play his cards right.

Once he was back in his car starting it up, he pulls off but the drug was on him heavy. That shit was the best blast he ever had in his life. The shit hasn't been stepped on. Craig reached for the box of blunts in his passenger seat, that were pre rolled. He found a note stuck to the box; it read, "Hustle by any means necessary no matter who you have to fuck over. Love Hurricane."

Craig threw the box back on the seat looking around to see who could have done this. He doesn't see Hurricane, but she'd sees him. As a car ran a red light, his car is knocked into a building. As she drove past him, she could hear him hollering for help.

Taz is fucked up behind all this shit; he doesn't know what to do without a plug or place to stay. He has a hundred thousand, yet the way he is used to living, it would not hold him long. Besides, he has to purchase a place to stay for his family.

Taz know Rashida would be pissed about the move. He sat in the office of the Rainbow Cloud looking at the insurance policy he has in his name. He is glad that fire coverage is a hundred thousand. That will put money back in his pocket after he bought a small house.

Alicia Howard Presents

Taz doesn't understand how his plan didn't go right. He cleaned out the safe, yanks a few wires out the fuse box, standing there watching it as it sparked and popped. Once he saw a small blaze, he got the hell out of there; it's time to kiss the Rainbow Cloud goodbye.

Alicia Howard Presents

Stacy has all her men in motion to supply the hood so she used her free time to look at her new, wonderful house. She never dreamt in a million years she would live this good at twenty. She is just a girl from the projects balling, out of control.

Stacy is thankful for her new big sister and family. She would handle the business while Hurricane ran around causing hell.

Alicia Howard Presents

Breeze is at home packing his bag. He going to New Jersey for a while, just until things mellows out. Taz has called telling him how things went at court; he couldn't believe that she didn't leave the man anything.

Well, he doesn't deserve it nor earn the shit. Breeze couldn't deal with Taz's problems at the moment because he has his own. He found another note in his car, reading, *"Sex is never safe with a nasty girl. Love Hurricane."* He doesn't know what the note meant, but whomever is doing this is now leaving

Hurricane's name on it. Breeze couldn't deal anymore.

He gatherers his bags to take to his car but was stopped dead in his tracks. Another note is on the inside of his door as if someone was in his house with him. He quickly reads the note. *"You can run, but you can't hide. Love Hurricane."* Breeze passed out instantly.

CHAPTER 40

Wesley is tired of Hurricane sneaking out, so he came with her tonight. She parked the car in the same spot as he sat there and waited for her. The place where he parked gave him a clear view of the house if she needs help.

When she went in, the house was still clean, shockingly. She did her normal things before anyone woke up. Hurricane was in the bathroom about to run water after setting out Taz's clothing again. She hears footsteps not big enough to be Taz nor small enough to be children. She knows it's Rashida this was

Alicia Howard Presents

the moment she has been waiting on. She stumbles in to the dimly lit bathroom to use it.

Rashida looks at the toilet strangely; someone was one it. She stepped closer that's when she heard, "Hi" Rashida."

"Hurricane?" Rashida rubs her eyes more.

"Yup," Hurricane smiles.

"Are you real?" Hurricane know this hoe is dumb but not this dumb.

"Nope...BOO," Hurricane yells.

Rashida ran out the bathroom screaming "It's her, it her, its herrrrrrr."

Alicia Howard Presents

Thank you for taking the time to read this book, I hope you enjoyed reading it as much as I enjoyed writing it.

Keep reading - it's fundamental.

38221303R00216

Made in the USA
San Bernardino, CA
02 September 2016